THE MAN WHO
TURNED INTO
HIMSELF

THE MAN WHO TURNED INTO HIMSELF

DAVID AMBROSE

ST. MARTIN'S PRESS
NEW YORK

ISBN 0-312-10497-9

First published in Great Britain by Jonathan Cape.

for Laurence

THE MAN WHO
TURNED INTO
HIMSELF

PART ONE

1

I LAY IN BED, listening to the silence of the house and trying to recall the dream that had woken me with such a start of fear. I remembered running through wide, battle-scarred streets under a flame-filled sky, but whatever demons had been pursuing me had already slipped back over the horizon into unconsciousness.

Anne was breathing softly at my side, miraculously undisturbed by the twisting and turning I must have been doing. I could tell I wasn't going to get back to sleep easily, so I slid out from under the covers, pulled on my slippers and robe, and padded downstairs.

There was still a smell of wood-smoke in the living room, but all that remained of the evening's log fire was a pile of white ash in the hearth. I pulled back a curtain and looked out. It was a clear Connecticut night with a touch of frost under a nearly full moon. In that light our rambling, half-wild garden became a place of secrets and enchantment, conjuring up memories of the cozy, old-fashioned children's stories that my grandparents used to read to me at Christmas around a roaring fire in their Devon farmhouse.

My father worked for a firm of heating engineers in London. When I was ten, he was offered a job in Philadelphia. Neither he nor my mother ever really settled there, and as soon as he retired they moved back to the south of England, which they still thought of as home. But by that time I was at Princeton, and in love.

Anne and I lived together for almost four years before

we married, then waited another two years before deciding that we could afford to start a family. Charlie was just a few months old when we found this house. We had both loved it from the moment we first saw it. We wanted more children and lots of space to have them. We also wanted to live outside the city. The loan we took out was bigger than we could afford, but we gambled on being able to make the payments, and so far we had been lucky. In fact I sometimes felt that we were luckier, and happier, than we had any right to expect. Now Anne was pregnant again, just as we'd planned.

I shivered, suddenly aware of the cold, and let the curtain fall back. Had the nightmare that woke me come from the fear that good things were given only to be taken away, as though by some sadistic Manichaean principle? Did I really believe in that kind of a universe?

Maybe I did. Somewhere.

I switched on a lamp in a reflex effort to push these thoughts away, then debated whether to pour myself a whiskey or go through to the kitchen and make a hot cup of chocolate. I settled for the chocolate because I'd drunk enough with dinner and wanted a clear head for the morning.

As I stirred the pan on the stove I became aware of someone watching me. Anne was leaning against the door frame, arms folded, feet crossed. She wore a robe like mine. We had bought them together. Her short, dark hair was tousled and her eyes, normally wide with an expression between surprise and laughter, were sleepy.

'I'll have whatever you're having,' she said.

'I'm sorry I woke you.'

'You didn't. The empty bed did.' Her eyes followed me to the fridge for more milk and to the shelf for more chocolate. 'What's worrying you? Are you afraid that now you've made up your mind, they're going to change theirs?'

'It's not about tomorrow,' I responded, with a touch of impatience in my voice. She arched an eyebrow sceptically. 'Of course not,' stifling a yawn and smiling at the same time.

'It's just a coincidence that you're up at 3 am making yourself comfort drinks.'

'Everything's set for tomorrow. The meeting's only a formality.'

She came towards me, slipped her arms over my shoulders and looked into my eyes, first one then the other, the way she always did. 'All I want is to be sure you're doing it because *you* want to, not because you think you should for me, Charlie and the bump.' The 'bump' was her pregnancy that didn't even show yet. She pushed it against me, rubbing softly.

'Are you accusing me of putting my family before personal preferences?'

'It's possible.'

'You're calling me a wimp?'

'Yes.' She pressed her face to mine as my hands slid under her robe. 'Rick,' she murmured, and didn't have to say any more. I hoisted her gently up and she locked her legs around my waist. Somehow I managed to switch off the stove before I carried her out. I almost tripped on her robe as she dropped it, wobbled painfully on one of Charlie's Ninja Turtles on the stairs, and gave a muffled curse as I banged my elbow on the door at the top. 'It's never like this in the movies,' I said, lowering her, and myself with her, to the bed.

'No,' she whispered, a little breathless even though I was the one doing all the work, 'there isn't room in those narrow seats.'

Charlie woke us ten minutes before the alarm went off to say that he could hear Gummo, our Siamese cat, stuck on the roof again. I pulled on an old tracksuit and climbed into the chilly loft to let him in through a skylight. Charlie waited anxiously where I'd told him to on the landing, circled by Harpo, his mongrel terrier, who pierced the air with a repeated nervous yelp.

The cat was really freaked by something. I tried everything

5

I knew to get him in, including coaxing, cajoling, and even having Charlie run down to get his food bowl filled with his favourite breakfast. It was no good; the wretched animal just prowled up and down the tiles, making plaintive meowing noises and staying carefully beyond my reach. I realised I was going to have to go out and get him. I hauled myself up through the skylight, inwardly reflecting that domestic bliss, like most kinds of happiness, had its shortcomings.

Climbing out on to a sloping roof of very old tiles before the overnight frost had completely thawed was not the cleverest thing I've ever done. The cat seemed to sense the danger and ran for his life, terrified that I might pick him up and then fall, still clutching him.

I don't think I would have fallen at all if the cat hadn't turned and lashed out at me, lips drawn back in a snarl and claws extended, when I went after him. I'm pretty agile and I was moving with care, but I just wasn't ready for this reaction from a cat who, I swear, spends half his life sleeping on my desk, and the other half curled up on my lap whenever I sit down to read. I cursed him, and suddenly I heard a scream. Not my voice. Anne's.

As the world began to spin, I saw her terrified face in the skylight I'd just climbed out of. Only then did I realise that the world was spinning because I was falling.

It was one of those moments where reality hangs suspended. It's not even that things happen in slow motion. They're both happening and not happening at the same time. Events are kept at arm's length by a protective barrier of shock and denial. You think thoughts you don't have time to think. You realise in a detached, purely intellectual way that something awful is happening, but without really touching you.

Then your imagination goes to work. You have a flash of yourself in a wheelchair for the rest of your life. Even worse, on your back, a quadriplegic in an orthopaedic bed.

Suddenly . . . I'm not absolutely sure about this, but I think I heard myself laughing. It was all too absurd to be taken seriously. It couldn't be true!

6

Anne's scream continued to ring in my ears as I pitched off the roof, turning in space. I could hear Charlie's cry and the dog's panicky barking in the loft behind her. But they were wrong, surely, to be alarmed. It couldn't happen. It couldn't!

I didn't know much for a while after I landed. I didn't black out, but time stopped.

Then I felt the life begin to flow back into all the parts of my body. Mentally I checked them off, one by one. Things moved. I was whole.

By the time Anne reached me I was on my feet, picking chunks of the evil-smelling compost into which I'd fallen off my tracksuit.

I inspected myself in the long bathroom mirror as I stepped out of the shower. I'd have a bruise or two, but nothing worse. The fact that I was in good shape, thanks to a vigorous workout several times a week, had probably helped. At least I'd landed with a certain degree of physical co-ordination.

How remote it seemed already, that appalling knowledge that everything hung in the balance. Suppose I'd cracked my head open? Another couple of feet either way and it would have been like a coconut against concrete. I peered into the eyes between the dark mop of hair and the white foam as I began to shave. How must brain damage feel, from the inside? You must know there's something terribly wrong, but you're not sure what. Maybe every so often you get a kind of oblique flash of the appalling truth: *you're* what's wrong. You're a freak, not quite human. People pity you, but above all they fear you, because you have become their nightmare.

I closed my eyes and forced myself to think of something else. Moments later I was heading downstairs for breakfast. As I entered the warm kitchen that smelled of coffee, eggs and toast, Charlie took up the refrain he had been chanting non-stop and with much hilarity ever since it happened.

'Daddy fell in the doo-doos, daddy fell in the doo-doos . . . !'

I drove down tree-lined lanes, working through the intricate network of back roads that joined the highway at the last possible point before entering the city. The radio was on, but I couldn't have told you two minutes afterwards what the headlines on the news had been. The day, which had already started out dramatically, would, if all went well, be an important one for me.

My company, Hamilton Publications Inc., had set up in business nearly six years earlier, with just myself, my assistant Marcie, and two others. Our specialist publications ranged from a literary review to a newsletter for professional caterers. One of our earliest efforts had become a must with every wine grower on the west coast. There was a bi-monthly that no gallery owner could afford to be without. High school science departments subscribed in their thousands to *Particle/Wave*, a digest and update of progress in the new physics, too simple for genuine researchers but too technical for the layman.

I or one of the team would spot what looked like a gap in the market and then check it out demographically. Nine times out of ten we came up with compelling reasons to drop the idea; but that one time out of ten would add another title to our list.

After a while total strangers started calling up or writing in with ideas. Three of them had, within weeks, found themselves allocated office space and running their own brain-child. We devised a profit share scheme so that they felt they were working as much for themselves as for the firm.

About a year ago we'd started to attract attention from the big boys. A couple of conglomerates had come sniffing around with buy-out offers, but I wasn't keen on going to work for somebody else. Essentially I'm a dabbler, an ideas man. I love nothing better than to spend days and sometimes weeks reading up on some topic that has caught my imagination. It can be nuclear physics or traffic control. I'm a kind of specialist in the eclectic; or 'totally lacking in intellectual focus' as they put it in college, where I did not distinguish myself.

Anyway, the business, at the point or the plateau it had reached, was a kind of natural extension of me, one that I didn't want to give up just yet, not even in return for a lot of money.

At the same time, it might have been nice to branch out in one or two other directions. For instance, I'll tell you something that may not have occurred to you. Do you want to know how people *really* are? How they're feeling, what they're saying, what they really mean? If you want to know what is truly going on in the world around you, don't read anything by journalists or sociologists or any kind of analyst. Don't even talk to cab drivers.

Read the trade papers. There's one for every trade and everything that likes to call itself a profession. The boasts ring so hollow and the anxieties stare so searingly through that the truth, unspoken, hits you like a sledgehammer. The trades are the code books to what's happening and where we're going. I wanted to start my own string of them. And try something, I don't know . . . new.

My lawyer, Harold, had begun making inquiries about possible sources of finance, hence the meeting at the bank. Anne had made me promise to call her and report as soon as we were through. She was taking Charlie into town some time late morning for a friend's birthday party that was to begin with a movie outing. After that she would be working at home all afternoon. She organised a charity that ran shelters for the homeless. It was unpaid work and she was fully aware that the help they offered was a drop in the ocean. She used to joke that it was a perfect job for a knee-jerk liberal: well-meaning, pious, and ultimately ineffectual. She'd been a journalist before having Charlie, a good one with a promising future. She could have gone back to it but chose not to. I think she was prouder of what she was doing than . . .

The sound of the horn reached me from a long, long way away. I don't know where my mind had been. Not consciously going over all the things I have just been setting down. All I know is that I suddenly seemed to come out of a daydream to find a huge truck bearing down on me, horn blaring and lights flashing.

I swung the wheel to the right, and still don't know how I managed to miss him. The car skidded and stalled and came to a halt half on and half off the road. For a while I couldn't do anything except sit there shaking and feeling a clammy, cold perspiration all over me. Eventually I pulled myself together and drove off, hunched over the wheel in fierce concentration, heart still pounding.

Even by the time I'd parked in my numbered space in the lot behind our building, I was still shaky. To miss death twice in one morning was too close for me. I had this jolt of superstition about things coming in threes. It was a few minutes before I got out of the car and headed into the building – big, square, turn-of-the-century. It closed itself around me that morning like an old friend, familiar and reassuring.

I took the elevator to the sixth floor, where we occupied half the available space. I pushed open the door with its modest logo: 'Hamilton Publications Inc.' Jigger, the receptionist, smiled up from her desk and the day's first cup of coffee and said good morning. I walked through to my corner office, greeting on the way the four men and two women who were in before me because they had deadlines to meet by the end of the day. The others would be in soon if they weren't tied up seeing contributors or working at home. Marcie always knew where everybody was if I needed to talk to them.

'Harold called to ask can you pick him up at his office so you can talk on the way over.' Marcie was checking off my messages with her customary efficiency.

'Okay,' I said, 'tell him I'll stop by at ten after.'

10

'And he said,' she gave a puzzled frown, 'that I wasn't under any circumstances to let you out on the roof. What does that mean?'

I sighed. 'It means that he called home before he called here.' I told her the story, which kept her giggling on and off for the next twenty minutes while we dealt with the morning's mail.

Harold had been my best friend ever since I came to America. He had lived across the street and quickly took me under his wing, introduced me around, taught me to play baseball, and made excuses for my accent until it blended into a reasonable facsimile of his own.

Now he was a lawyer, my lawyer, and a very clever one. I trusted him with everything, and he'd never let me down. He dreamed up contracts which were impeccably concise, yet loose enough to let the independent and sometimes eccentric people I worked with feel at ease. He'd knit together loans, mortgages and pension schemes and never dropped a stitch. He'd also fought and beaten a massive New York law firm that had been sent after us with a phony copyright claim by a conglomerate that meant to put us out of business.

He was just stepping out of his building as I pulled my lovingly restored '67 Mustang to the curb. I had anticipated the sly smile, the hint of mockery on his face.

'I want to know that you're feeling positive. Are you feeling positive?'

'Shut the door, Harold.'

'Just because your first bold leap of the day landed you in a pile of shit . . . '

'Yeah, yeah . . . '

' . . . doesn't mean the next one will necessarily do the same.'

I pulled out to re-join the traffic. 'It was just compost. You're as bad as Charlie.'

He sniffed the air ostentatiously. 'Still, another shower

might have been a good idea. Just kidding, relax. We're going to get everything we want this morning, I swear it.' He started to laugh. 'Boy, I'd like to have been there with a camera!'

I decided not to tell him about the near-miss with the truck.

'And what's all this about getting up in the middle of the night for comfort foods? Hot chocolate, my God!'

I wondered for a split second if Anne had also told him how and why I never got around to drinking it. Then I smiled. What if she had? He had become her friend just as much as mine. I was glad they got along so well.

The fact that Harold had never married had made Anne wonder briefly whether he was gay. But I couldn't believe that, if he was, I wouldn't have known. Besides, he'd never lacked girlfriends, some of them very beautiful, some of them very accomplished, many of them both. He was attractive to women in an easy-going, understated sort of way. He knew exactly who he was, didn't come on macho, never seemed to ask more than they were prepared to give. Besides, he was only my age – thirty-four. Time enough.

' . . . especially if Chuck Morgan starts "thinking out loud" the way he does,' I suddenly heard Harold saying. 'Don't get drawn into that. Just dig in and stick to what we agreed.'

'I'm sorry,' I said, 'I didn't quite get all of that.'

He looked at me. 'Where did I lose you?'

'From the top down to Chuck Morgan thinking out loud.'

Harold rolled his eyes. 'Forget it. What you don't know now it's too late to fix. Just nod and smile and let me do the talking.' He had glanced my way as he spoke, and suddenly I was acutely aware that he hadn't turned away. I avoided meeting his gaze, embarrassed and feeling almost guilty for some reason. There was an edge of concern in his voice when he spoke. 'Are you okay?'

'I'm fine.'

'You're sure you didn't land on your head . . . ?'

Bob Crossfield was a genial man with silver hair and a big shapeless body expertly streamlined by a carefully tailored suit. He crossed to us with hand extended as we were shown into his office. We sat in comfortable armchairs and a secretary appeared with coffee on a silver tray. Harold caught my eye, looking smug. He knew that this greeting from the bank president meant that we were well on our way to getting precisely the terms we wanted. I relaxed a little, but still felt uncharacteristically nervous, unable to pin my uneasiness on anything in particular.

After a few minutes of conversation Roy Gaines, Crossfield's assistant, came in to say that the rest of the team were assembled in the conference room. I started to get to my feet, but, as I did, something strange and alarming happened. It was as though something snapped, or burst, inside my head, giving me a sudden feeling of being hopelessly cut off from everything around me.

'A stroke!' was my first panic-stricken thought. 'Brain haemorrhage.' I knew that it could happen even to young and apparently healthy people. My fall that morning had maybe done more damage than I'd realised. I wanted to cry out for help, but no sound would come. The three men in the room with me had become distant, hazy figures, apparently unaware of my plight. Their voices slowed and mixed into a mechanical, meaningless drone, and my own breathing and heartbeat thundered in my ears. Instinctively I grabbed for my head, stumbled, and felt I was about to pitch full length on the floor.

Then, just as abruptly, everything returned to normal. Sound and vision popped back into focus as though nothing had happened. I realised at once that I hadn't made the exhibition of myself that I feared I had. The hand grab to my head became a polite cover for an improvised cough, the brief unsteadiness passed unnoticed. All the same I needed a moment to pull myself together, take a few deep breaths, get a grip. I asked for the men's room before going into the meeting. Gaines showed me to a panelled door in the back of the office.

The relief at finding myself alone for a moment was extraordinary, almost as though I was running from some enemy and suddenly found myself in sanctuary. Was I sick? Some kind of virus? I looked at my reflection in the mirror above the washbowl: perfectly normal, neither flushed nor pale. And yet I was suddenly feeling alternately hot and cold. I dowsed my face in water, dried it, and took another look. Nothing had changed. Except –

I spun around. There was no sign of anyone behind me, and yet I could swear – no, I *knew* – that I had seen a movement in the mirror. I turned back to it. Nothing. Had someone opened the door to make sure I was all right, then quickly withdrew? Surely I had locked it. I checked. I had.

So there was no one in the room. Just myself. And I was seeing things.

It seemed to me that this was one of those times when the best thing to do is go home, get into bed, and stay there. But whatever the reasons for my distracted jumpiness that morning – mental, physical, real or imaginary – I had an important meeting to get through, and get through it I would!

I gave my reflection one last, defiant glare, and turned to leave.

Seated around the long table in the panelled conference room were five men and one woman. We had all met at least once before, none the less Crossfield made introductions and we shook hands.

In front of each one of us was a water glass and carafe, plus a legal pad and felt-tipped pen with the bank's name on it. Also everyone was supplied with a copy of the bank's report on Hamilton Publications Inc., a tight little document full of words like growth curve, profit projection and all the rest of the jargon-riddled double-talk that experts use to dress up their guesswork. Crossfield made introductory remarks, I delivered a short prepared speech about how glad I was to be sitting around a table with them all, then began doodling on my legal pad as Harold launched into the details.

Obviously I knew every dot and comma of what was under discussion, but I remember being struck at one point by my remarkable lack of attention to what was actually being said. I thought as I glanced up that I caught an odd look in Bob Crossfield's eye. Chuck Morgan was also looking my way. He was only a couple of years older than me, but almost completely bald and with a tennis player's wiry physique. I put down the pen and made a show of paying close attention.

Crossfield asked me if I had anything to add to what Harold had said. I knew he would, and I said I hadn't. The discussion was then opened out to include the whole group. Sure enough Chuck Morgan started 'thinking out loud' in a direction which, if unchecked, would have significantly lowered the bank's risk and increased their control. Harold, with infinite grace, quickly circumvented him and looked to me for murmurs and nods of agreement, which I readily supplied. The 'thoughts' were abandoned.

Others had little to add, and it became clear that the meeting was indeed a formality, there to give its imprimatur to what had already been decided. I reached out to pour myself a glass of water. I don't know why but my mouth was suddenly very dry, my lips sticking together so that I felt if I had to speak the words would come out incoherently. It was as the glass was halfway to my mouth that I caught sight of what I had been doodling a few minutes ago.

I am not gifted artistically, and anything I draw usually resembles the work of one of those chimpanzees you see in learning experiments in TV documentaries. But I was startled by the clarity of what I was looking at now. I had drawn the same figure several times, first small then growing larger, as though approaching. It was the figure of a woman running.

She was holding out her arms as though reaching for something or someone. She was obviously in terror, and in the third sketch had fallen to her knees and was crawling. In the fifth she was stretched out on the ground, though still apparently trying to move. In the sixth she was pinned down like a specimen of some insect on a slide, or else crushed by some immense, unseen weight. The seventh sketch was a dark and horrible thing, a Goya-like glimpse of something too terrible to contemplate, an impression of pain, dismemberment and death.

'Rick? Rick!' Harold repeated my name louder. I must have been called upon to make some response, but I hadn't heard a thing. Without looking up I knew that all eyes were on me. A silence had fallen on the room. It was obvious to everyone that something was wrong.

The crash that the glass made as it slipped from my fingers was like an explosion. It was followed by the sound of my chair sliding back violently. By the time it hit the floor I was racing for the door, oblivious of the astonishment and alarm all around me.

But none of it mattered. All that counted was what was in my head, the knowledge that was suddenly planted there. Maybe 'planted' is the wrong word. It was knowledge unveiled, as though it had been there all along and I had been suppressing it.

At any rate I knew for sure, just as surely as though a voice had spoken, what it all meant.

Maybe even that isn't accurate. Maybe instead of knowing I was simply gripped by a compulsion. Instead of thinking I was responding, though without any knowledge of what I was responding to. I was propelled – yes, that was it, propelled – by a force that wasn't physical or even mental. What I was doing had to be done. It was stronger than conviction. It was inevitable.

And yet there was uncertainty. Not uncertainty of purpose, but of whether I could achieve what I knew I must attempt. If I had been stopped then and made to explain what I thought

I was doing, I'm not sure I would have been able to. All I knew was that the woman I had drawn was Anne. I knew she wasn't reaching out for me but for Charlie. I had drawn the desperation of a woman trying to save her child.

But from what?

Without knowing how I got there, I found myself in the underground parking lot with my car keys in my hand. As I drove out with squealing tyres I caught a glimpse of Harold and Roy Gaines, who must have followed me, waving at me to stop. I ignored them, as I ignored the flimsy wooden barrier that the startled gate man would have raised for me had I paused to hand over the validated parking ticket in my pocket. It scraped along the Mustang's hood, shattered the windshield, then flew off its hinge and spun towards the ceiling.

For some time – again I don't know how long – I must have driven with the opaque labyrinthine pattern of my shattered windshield blocking any view of where I was going. I remember that eventually I punched a fist through it – and found I was exactly where I expected to be, approaching a stop sign at an intersection of three roads. Ignoring the sign I swung through protesting traffic and took the first exit. Even then I didn't know where I was headed. I just knew that I was headed somewhere.

How I got away with so many infractions of the law in so short a space of time I shall never know. Speed and luck, I suppose. But even if there had been police cars chasing me with flashing lights and wailing sirens, I probably wouldn't have noticed. I doubt I would have noticed anything short of gunfire, with bullets thudding into the upholstery all around me. And maybe not even that.

Later, much later when I had time to reflect on it all, I went back over the road and measured the distance I drove that morning. It was exactly 3.9 miles from the exit of the bank parking lot to the spot where the traffic jam started. I don't remember any sense of frustration when I saw the long tailback starting under the bridge and winding up Pilgrim

17

Hill and out of sight. It was obvious that the road was totally blocked somewhere up ahead. What I don't know — honestly don't know despite the number of times I've tried to recall the moment — was whether I knew then what had happened; or whether I was still simply hurtling forward in an unthinking trance. Certainly there was no doubt in my mind by then about where I was going. I sprang from my car leaving the door open and the engine running, and started scrambling up the grassy slope to the left of the road. People watched me from below, wondering who this madman was, and where he had to be so urgently.

At the top of the slope, sweating, clothes torn and muddied, fingernails ripped and bleeding from the final hard-won, steepening yards of the climb, I stopped and looked towards the head of the jam. I knew exactly where it was, of course. But did I know *what* it was? From where I stood I couldn't see much aside from a general confusion, people running, a crowd forming, an odd scattering of vehicles that suggested an accident. I ran towards it as fast as I could.

There were a few token grunts and protests as I shouldered my way through to see what was at the centre of it all. But by then I think I knew. I had known for a split second in the conference room when I dropped the glass and ran out. I had glimpsed the awful thing that confronted me now, but the image had been pushed to the back of my mind while I negotiated the journey here. Now there was no turning from it.

A huge refrigerated rig, much larger than the one that had almost killed me that morning, had gone out of control and jumped the central divide. It had jackknifed and turned over. The back had sprung open and deep-frozen carcasses of meat were scattered everywhere. Beneath the vehicle a small car lay crushed. It was pale green and still, though only just, recognisable as the imported 'Deux Chevaux' that Anne had wanted ever since our first trip to Europe. They had stopped making that model, and it was a while before I found a specialist dealer who supplied me with one for her thirtieth birthday.

She had been so happy, thrilled like a child, when she came downstairs and found a key on the table with a huge bow attached to it, then saw the car through the window parked outside. I had put a picnic hamper on the back seat, filled with French bread and champagne and a bottle of wine and some foie-gras and a birthday cake with her name on it. All we had to do was drive out to a spot I'd already chosen and . . .

. . . and now she lay dying, trapped, bleeding, pushed back as though recoiling in some impossible cartoon-like exaggeration of shocked outrage. Except this was no cartoon, and no exaggeration. It was simply the literal truth of what massive, unstoppable force had done to her.

I don't know whether I cried out, said anything, in any way communicated who I was, but people suddenly made way for me, let me go forward, lowering their voices, bringing a strange stillness to the scene.

A man was on one knee, struggling with what remained of the car's rear door. If I saw his face I don't remember it. All I remember is a broad back with a cheap grey suit stretched tight across it as his fleshy shoulders worked. He had a thick neck with a roll of fat above the collar. His hair was reddish-brown, short and greasy, brushed back flat on his head. And suddenly, as he turned, he had my son in his arms.

Charlie was deathly white but alive. And, I realised as he clung to me and I felt the sobs racking my body, he was unhurt.

I don't remember if I handed him to someone or if someone prized him gently from me. At moments like that there is, I think, an almost psychic understanding between people. Things are said, things are done, without reflection and with a sureness that is lacking in more normal times. Charlie was taken from me to be cared for, and he knew this was right. He didn't cry, he didn't cling, he knew what he must do.

I turned to Anne. She could move her head only slightly, barely more than an inch; but her eyes made the rest of the journey to meet mine, and she saw her own death in my anguish.

Her lips moved and I bent closer. But she wasn't trying to speak; only to give me a faint last smile, a loving goodbye, a reassurance that she knew and accepted what was happening.

The agony of not being able to hold her as she died was unbearable, but she was trapped in a vice-like coffin of steel that left me outside, a helpless onlooker. Somewhere distantly I heard a siren drawing close, then a voice saying it would be hours before they could cut her free.

Only we didn't have hours. These were our last minutes. Perhaps seconds.

I reached for her face, almost afraid to touch in case the contact brought back the physical pain which she seemed mercifully to have slipped beyond. But she gave a faint sigh, almost of pleasure, as my fingertips caressed her cheek and lips. I leaned forward to kiss her, but her eyes glazed over. Where there had been stillness there was now only the emptiness of death.

Somehow, as I slumped forward with a howl of unfathomable loss that seemed to come from somewhere so deep in my being that it was almost outside of me, my hand found hers. She must have thrown it up, instinctively trying to protect herself from the impact, and now it protruded, fingers splayed, from the appalling inch-wide gap between the dash and the seat on which she lay.

The people around us let me be, knowing that my grief must have this moment, letting the sobs shake free unhindered from my body. Then, very gently, I felt hands taking hold of me, pulling me away.

I said yes, let them, this is right. Don't spoil the dignity of her going with your own self-centred torment. Just do what must be done. Think of your son, he is alone, he needs you.

But I had reckoned without the rage, the senseless, aching

20

rage that swept through me like a flame. Against my will I hunched forward, clung to what remained of her, my eyes shut tight against a truth I could not tolerate. As though in slow, slow motion my head arched back and I roared into the blackness of my inner universe: a roar of terrifying, primal, primitive defiance.

That was when I felt the movement in her hand. I didn't open my eyes at first. I knew that I was dreaming and didn't want to wake from the forlorn, illusory hope that I was wrong, that she still lived.

And then I heard her voice. 'Get me out of here before this thing rolls over. Richard, help me! Get me out of here, quick!'

I looked. Her eyes were open, locked on mine, wide and full of fear but fighting, brave. I was a sleepwalker, a passive, stunned spectator of the next few moments.

Help was everywhere. Strong men lifting, straining, carrying her to safety. She was alive! Cut, bruised, in shock, but living, standing there unaided suddenly, before me.

Somehow I swam forward through the dizzying waves of unreality that swept over me. I took her in my arms. She was solid, warm, and real. It seemed impossible, but she was alive!

It was Anne who took control now, calming me, telling me over and over that everything was all right. She stroked my face, her dark eyes pouring reassurance into mine, soothing me with gentle child-like noises of affection. I tried to speak but couldn't. She put her fingers to my lips. Don't try. It's all right. We're together. Everything is all right. We're safe.

Suddenly, almost guilty at having been so caught up in my own emotion, I remembered Charlie. I turned and called his name, expecting him to run to us, to be swept into our arms and hugged and kissed and reassured that there was nothing more to fear.

But no child ran from the surrounding group of silent onlookers. I called his name again. Blank stares, silently

21

onlookers. I called his name again. Blank stares, silently exchanged looks of puzzlement were all that met my gaze.

I turned to Anne. 'Where is he? He was here, safe.'

'Who?'

With a chill that reached my soul I saw in her eyes the same uncertain, half-frightened incomprehension that was all around me. 'Charlie! Our son Charlie! They got him out! He wasn't hurt! I held him. Charlie!' I was screaming suddenly, turning wildly, calling for our son who had vanished into thin air.

'Richard! Richard!' Anne was holding me, trying to calm me, fighting to restrain my helpless, flailing arms. 'Don't, Richard, don't! Don't do this!'

'Where is he? I couldn't have been wrong? Where is he? Where's our son.'

'Richard! Richard!' She shook me, made me look at her, fixed my eyes with her own determined, anxious gaze. 'We have no son. I don't know what you're saying. We have no son.'

Again I felt the waves of blackness sweeping over me. I fought to keep my balance, to hang on to my sanity in the face of this absurdity. My head spun one way, then another, taking in the groups of baffled, murmuring onlookers. What were they to do? Who was this crazy man screaming for a child whom only he seemed to imagine had existed?

Then I saw the accident, the jack-knifed rig and the car trapped under it.

But the car was no longer Anne's car. In the grotesque tangle of metal, glass and leather I recognised the colour and distorted outline of my own car. It was my dark blue Mustang that had collided with the truck.

Something warm and liquid ran down my face, catching the corner of my eye. I reached up and my hand reappeared in front of me soaked in blood.

I looked down at my clothes. They were not the same clothes I had been wearing. Nor was the expensive-looking, though now torn and stained grey trouser-suit that Anne

22

had on, anything that I had seen on her before. She had never owned a suit like that. And yet it was Anne looking at me with concern and fear, as though I was in some terrible trouble and she didn't know how to help me.

There was a flurry of movement in the crowd surrounding us. Two men pushed through in the uniform of paramedics, unfolding a stretcher as they came. In their eyes I saw the trained, alert professional calm of people schooled in dealing with emergencies. They were coming for me, preparing to take care of this panic-stricken, hysterical victim of ... of what?

As the blackness finally overwhelmed me and I began falling, the last thing I felt was strong hands grabbing me before I hit the ground.

2

THE DRUGS THEY gave me had the effect of leaving me suspended between drowsiness and oblivion for what seemed an age. Each time I surfaced a nurse checked my temperature and pulse and gave me something to drink. It must have happened half a dozen times before I felt strong enough to push myself up on one elbow and demand to know where I was. The name of the hospital meant nothing, but that was hardly surprising as I had no reason to be familiar with all the hospitals in the city.

A doctor – young, skinny, with a pursed mouth and a nose that pecked at the air as he talked – came in and gave me a cursory examination. He said I had been unconscious for thirty-six hours and would have to remain there a while yet. His manner irritated me beyond endurance. It was as though he tried to compensate for his lack of physical presence by adopting a Gestapo-like peremptoriness which brooked neither argument nor question. I cut him short, swung my feet to the floor, and announced I was leaving at once. My efforts to push him aside must have been comical, since I had barely the strength to stand. Nevertheless I put up as good a fight as I could and we wound up struggling noisily on the floor. I had a brief worm's eye view of the door bursting open and white-shod feet hurrying to his rescue. Then I felt the jab of a needle in my arm and sank, still struggling, once more into darkness.

When I woke, Anne was sitting by my bed. She looked drawn and pale and I had the impression she had been there for some time. I tried to sit up, but she restrained me gently with a hand on my shoulder. 'Please, darling, don't. Just relax, you'll be out of here soon – but not if you start a fight every time you wake up.'

I settled back obediently and looked at her. There must have been something accusatory in my gaze because she shifted uneasily on her chair, then went on with a hint of apology in her voice. 'I know you're in shock, but please try to stay calm and don't make trouble. For my sake, please!' I just looked at her. She leant closer and went on quickly, as though afraid we were about to be interrupted. 'We were lucky, it could have been far worse. No one was badly hurt. All you have to do is show them you're all right and they'll discharge you.'

'For God's sake,' I hissed, 'tell me what's going on. What happened to Charlie?'

'Oh, Richard . . . ' Her eyes filled with tears and she bit the corner of her lower lip.

'And why d'you keep calling me Richard? What *is* all this?'

She stifled a sob and wiped underneath her eye with the back of her fingers. 'I'm sorry,' I said, 'I didn't mean – '

She shook her head. 'It's all right.' It was then that I noticed she was wearing her hair differently, pulled straight and tied at the back. Also there was something about her clothes: they were more severe somehow, as though she was trying to be someone else. I was about to make a comment when a nurse entered and, eyeing me sternly, held open the door for a doctor – a different one this time, older, but built like a marine and with a greying crew-cut. He was perfectly pleasant, however: relaxed, slow-speaking, and with a hint of irony in his manner.

'I know you feel strongly about getting out of here . . . ' he was shining a light in my eyes, first one, then the other. 'It shouldn't take more than a day or two.'

'There is nothing wrong with me.'

'Didn't say there was, did I? How many fingers am I holding up?'

'Three.'

'Good.'

'It's not good, it's ridiculous!'

'Hey, it's a wonder you can remember which way is up after all the stuff you've had shot into you.' He picked up my chart and made a note on it.

'I didn't ask to have anything shot into me!'

'We volunteered – figured you'd appreciate it later.'

I looked over at Anne. 'I want to see Harold right now.'

Crew-cut raised an eyebrow. 'Harold?'

'His lawyer,' Anne explained.

'Ah. Sure, see anyone you want.'

'Get Harold over here,' I said with emphasis.

She looked unhappy. 'Harold's in New York on business.'

'Since when?'

'Ten days.'

I took a moment to absorb this. 'That's not possible! I haven't been here ten days.' I looked up at crew-cut. 'How long have I been here?'

'Forty-eight hours.'

I turned back to Anne. She flinched at the puzzlement and anger she must have seen in my face. 'You know Harold's not away,' I almost shouted. 'I was with him just before the accident. He told me he talked to you on the phone that morning!'

Anne was biting her lower lip again, fighting back tears. Crew-cut's gaze had been switching back and forth between us. Now he stepped in to take over.

'Mrs Hamilton, there's nothing to seriously worry about. Your husband's going to be fine.' He wanted her out of the room. She took the hint and came over to kiss me. We looked at each other a moment, then she put her arms around me and held me close. I felt a pang of guilt that I had, however indirectly, accused her of betraying me in some strange way that I didn't yet understand. I didn't want her to leave. She was my anchor in a world gone mad.

As though reading my thoughts, she pulled back a little

and looked searchingly into my eyes. For a moment everything was all right. I knew this gesture. This was familiar,
this was real. 'I'll be back soon,' she whispered. 'I love you.'

'I know. I love you.' I returned the squeeze she had
given my hand. 'I'm okay.'

Then she was gone, quickly, not wanting to look back.
Crew-cut, who had remained discreetly on one side, now
regarded me with professional amiability from the foot of
my bed. 'Look,' he started, 'some people get the wrong idea
about this when the idea's first put to them, but I'm going
to do it anyway.' I waited. 'I can't find a damn thing wrong
with you physically. How would you feel about seeing a
psychiatrist? We have somebody here who's quite special.
I know you'd – '

'*You* see the fucking psychiatrist!' The force of my response
surprised me, but not apparently him. He didn't even blink.

'Like I said, most people get the wrong idea. They think
seeing a psychiatrist means admitting they're crazy. That's
not so.'

'I'm perfectly well aware of that,' I said testily, but keeping
my voice down now. 'I'm not entirely uneducated.' I paused,
then added grudgingly: 'I'm sorry I shouted.'

'That's okay. I know all this is a pain in the ass for
you. We're only trying to help.'

I sighed and leaned back on my pillows. 'If it'll do any
good, I'll see the shrink. All I want is to get out of here.'

The young woman who entered my room an hour later
was alone. She was also blind. She used her white cane to
find the chair by the side of my bed, sat down, and told me
her name was Emma Todd. She said if it was all right with
me she would call me Richard, and I was to call her Emma.
I said why didn't she call me Rick, like everybody else did.
She seemed to reflect on this for a moment, then said: 'Okay.
Rick.'

I don't know why I was so surprised to come across a

blind psychiatrist. In a way I suppose one thinks of it as a uniquely watching profession, though truly it's much more of a listening one. Certainly Emma Todd listened with an attentive stillness that was at first unnerving. But because of the freedom her blindness gave me to watch her without self-consciousness, I quickly began to feel at ease.

Although she struck me as plain, almost homely, in appearance, I realised the longer I looked at her that she had a face of considerable natural beauty. The bone structure was classical and the skin, untouched by make-up, flawless. But the short, straight brown hair did nothing to enhance it; and the dead, staring eyes, which were of a blue so pale as to be almost cataract-white, gave it a flatness which would not normally have merited a second glance. I guessed she was probably about my age but looked older. Also I suspected she had been blind since birth, as her whole posture had the awkwardness of someone unacquainted with visual grace.

Although our conversation had a casual, almost desultory quality, I remained on the alert, fully aware that she wasn't there for small talk but was making a diagnosis, noting my every phrase and careful circumlocution in search of some clue to my condition. I in my turn was trying to telegraph condition normal with every word I uttered. It was, I quickly learned, an oddly difficult, if not impossible, task. She was aware of this and her lips parted in a curiously endearing smile.

'Look,' she said, 'I know what you're doing, and you don't have to. I'm not trying to catch you out. Just talk as you would with a friend.'

'I'll try,' I said. 'You can't blame me for feeling just a little suspicious.'

She laughed, a light, unserious sound which made me like her more. 'Tell me about Charlie.'

'I'd rather not,' I said. 'Talking about Charlie seems to have got me into enough trouble already.'

'That's no reason for pretending he doesn't exist if you believe he does.'

I was silent. How could I pretend that my son didn't exist? Yet what was I supposed to say? Suddenly a sound came out of me that I didn't recognise at first. I wasn't even aware that it was coming from me. And then I realised: I was weeping.

She made no attempt to comfort me, no words of reassurance, no hand reaching for mine. She just let me go on for a while until I was quiet, then said: 'That's enough for now. You're tired. I'll come back tomorrow, you'll find it easier then.' She was halfway to the door, white stick probing the air for obstacles, before I spoke.

'Emma . . . ?'

'Yes?' She stopped, turned partially, seeking me with her ears I realised, not her eyes.

'Just tell me one thing. Am I being held here? I mean, against my will?'

Her reply had a simple directness that I was grateful for. 'Yes, in a sense. This isn't a psychiatric hospital, just a special unit in a general one. We persuaded your wife to sign you in for your own safety. But don't worry, the law doesn't allow us to keep you for more than three days without a review by an assessment panel, and I don't think they'll find grounds to hold you. You're suffering post-shock trauma. It's not unusual, although the form it's taken in your case is a little out of the ordinary. The best thing you can do is sleep. I'll see you in the morning. If you need anything, you'll find a buzzer by your bed.'

'Yes, all right, thank you.' She went out. There was a pause, then I heard someone lock the door behind her. I suddenly felt more wretched than I had ever in my life. I gazed at the window. All I could see was sky. There were no bars, but I could see the glass was thick, and there were catches to prevent it opening more than a few inches. I was overwhelmed by a combination of exhaustion, despair and the residue of whatever, as crew-cut put it, they had 'shot into' me. I fell into sleep as the only escape from the nightmare that my life had become.

From the light outside my window it must have been early evening when I woke. I buzzed for help in getting to the tiny bathroom that adjoined my room. At least I was being spared the humiliation of urinating into bottles and struggling on to bedpans. Afterwards they brought me something to eat – I was surprisingly hungry – and then a nurse came in pushing a cabinet on wheels from which she measured out a handful of pills into a small plastic cup. She poured me a glass of water and told me to swallow them. I debated refusing, but decided not to make trouble. I did something I must have seen a hundred times in movies but never thought would work in real life: I kept the pills in my mouth, swallowed the water, and turned away from her as though pretending to go to sleep, hiding my bulging cheeks. I heard her go out, lock the door, and realised that she had suspected nothing. I spat the pills into my hand and hid them underneath the mattress.

That little triumph gave a much-needed boost to my self-confidence. I began to feel, if only slightly, once more in control of events. Looking back, I suspect that, ironically, that was the moment when I actually began to lose what little control I still had.

Throwing off the bed covers I swung my feet to the floor and tried to stand unaided, and found that I could. The discovery flooded my whole system with an adrenalin-charged high. I felt suddenly that nothing could stop me. My one thought was to escape. Somehow my mind had convinced itself that if only I could reach the outside world I would find everything as it was, and the insanity of the recent past would be left behind in this sterile white cell.

As I thought, the window was fixed to open no more than a few inches, and even if the glass had been breakable I could not have risked the noise. However, I could see I was on the top floor of an L-shaped modern building which seemed to be near the edge of the hospital grounds. I had already noticed a trapdoor in the ceiling of the bathroom. Standing with one foot on the hand basin and the other on the lavatory flush tank, I managed with some effort to force it open and haul myself up into the darkness.

I made a discovery that night that has stayed with me ever since. I discovered how easy it is to get away with murder. Not literally, of course; I didn't kill anybody to get out of that place. But there I was one minute in my hospital-issue smock, bare feet and not a cent on me, scrambling around in the loft in search of a way down; and the next I was flagging down a cab and directing it to Long Chimneys. I was quite pleased with the way I looked – tweed jacket, grey flannels, Oxford loafers. Some doctor was going to be very upset when he got back to the locker room that night. Never mind, everything would be returned, including the money I had taken from some woman's purse that had been left for an instant just off the main reception area: I wasn't a thief.

Inevitably Long Chimneys was the first place they would look for me when my escape was discovered, but for the time being I had the advantage of surprise, and I had to talk to Anne alone. I had the cab drop me about a quarter of a mile from the house, which I approached on foot. There were lights on but no signs of unusual activity – no police cars, ambulances, men lurking in the shadows. It was still possible that my escape had not been noted, but there was no time to waste. Through the hedge (which I noticed with a perverse sense of irrelevance was more in need of a trim than I recalled) I could see that the curtains of our living room were open. I eased my way around until I could see in clearly, hoping to find Anne alone. What I did see was something that I was entirely unprepared for.

His back was to me and my first thought was that it must be Harold. Then he moved to pick up a newspaper and I realised he was no one I had ever seen. A woman came in, also a stranger. They spoke a few words, then she called off into the kitchen. Mesmerised, I moved along the wall and around the corner, and through the kitchen window saw two children aged about ten and twelve. They were dressed for bed and chasing noisily around the table with a large black and white English sheepdog.

I must have stayed there for some time, gazing in at those strangers; and at, I now realised, that furniture, those paintings on the wall, that huge television dominating the room, all of which had nothing to do with me or my life there with Anne and our son. Someone had taken over our house and totally wiped out every trace of our ever having lived there.

That was when I became aware of the dog's frantic barking. The sound seemed to come at first from a great distance, then I realised that I was standing right up against a window, and the animal was scrabbling to get at me from the other side, only inches away. Instinctively I started to run, headed for the road. But I only got to the corner of the house when the man I had seen inside met me, rifle in hand, and looking like nothing in the world would give him more pleasure than to kill me. I put up my hands and tried to explain that I meant no harm. He told me to shut the fuck up and marched me at gunpoint in through my own front door.

His wife was on the stairs, white-faced and frightened, ushering the children to safety. He told her to call the police. Her hands shook as she dialled 911.

Through the door into the living room I was aware of the big-screen television on too loud. A newscaster was announcing the death of some public figure whose name meant nothing to me. Then they ran some archive film from the early sixties. It was peripheral to the situation I was in, but suddenly it jumped to centre stage and seized my whole attention. They were running some film of the first President Kennedy, Jack Kennedy. It was a scene in Dallas somehow connected with the person who had just died. I watched with growing disbelief, and at the same time the first glimmerings of understanding, as the scene unfolded.

I saw President Jack Kennedy assassinated in an open car

32

alongside his wife on a sunny November day in 1963. The whole thing was presented as established history, a footnote from the past.

But as I and the whole world knew, Jack Kennedy had not been killed that day. True, somebody had taken a shot at him and missed, and had never been caught. Jack Kennedy served out his full term and was still alive. So was his brother Bobby who served one term as President after him.

And suddenly I knew. I knew what had happened.

I didn't understand.

But I knew.

The trip to the police station, the questions, the statements, all passed me by as little more than background noise. It was as though the whole world was just a television left on in the corner of the room, and the room was my head. It must have seemed to the cops that I was in a daze, but my mind was racing so fast I had to make a conscious effort not to cry out from the almost physical pain of it.

I don't know if they suspected something and called the hospital, or if the hospital had put out a warning by then that a patient was missing. At any rate I wasn't surprised to see two muscular male nurses arrive. I was resigned to going back. I was resigned by then to things I had never thought in my wildest dreams I might ever have to contemplate. My only concern was how to tell the truth without labelling myself a lunatic. I was turning over and over in my mind possible ways of beginning, thinking of people whose confidence I must win and whose help I would need. It amazes me, looking back, that I was so calm. But it was the calm of utter panic. I was frozen by the recognition of my situation like a rabbit in the headlights of a car.

A familiar voice pierced my absorption, and I turned to see Harold arguing with two cops at the desk. He looked like he had come straight from the airport, coat over his arm, bag at his feet.

Then I saw Anne pushing past him, her eyes on mine as she hurried towards me. All the little things that had bothered me about her last time I saw her didn't bother me any more. It all made sense now, if 'sense' was the right word; it was the only word I could think of. The idea of all that nonsense making sense made me laugh suddenly. Anne's face, already distraught from worry, took on such a look of alarm that I immediately felt guilty. I held her to me, assuaging her obvious pain with my leaden inner numbness.

'You have to give back the clothes, I've made good the money, and they won't press charges for theft.' I realised Harold was speaking to me.

'But what am I going to wear?' I heard myself saying in the dismayed tone of a perfectly reasonable man asked to do an unreasonable thing.

'Don't worry, we'll take care of that. Just say you agree.'

'Of course I agree,' I replied, adding: 'I only took them because — '

'Don't say any more,' Harold cut me off, holding up the palm of his hand. 'That's all I need.' He returned to his negotiations at the desk.

I looked down at Anne, and she met my gaze with a mixture of concern and puzzlement at my apparent calm. 'It's all right,' I said, 'I'm not crazy. I'll explain everything later.'

Of course 'explain' was the one thing I couldn't do. I could describe what was happening but not explain it — yet. Or maybe there was no difference. At that moment the distinction didn't bother me. All I felt was a flood of relief that I was able to function. 'It's all right,' I told myself, 'just take one step at a time and you'll get out of this.'

Again, looking back, I think I was afraid even to try to look further ahead than that. Had I done so I would have lost my precarious sense of balance and fallen off the tightrope into madness. It was strange, and also fascinating, to find myself so poised between two worlds. Or, more accurately, four: the world I had come from and this; and the worlds of sanity and madness.

Harold came back and drew us both aside, explaining in hushed clear tones what must be done. It was reassuring to have him there taking care of things. I realised not for the first time what a good lawyer, and good friend, he was. 'I can make a deal to get the trespass charges dropped and – maybe – get you released into Anne's custody. But you'll have to answer some questions. I've got a friend of mine coming over, a psychiatrist. If you can convince him that you're rational we'll get a provisional order – I've already called Judge Strickland – letting you go home.' He looked at me a moment searchingly. 'Can you handle that?'

'Absolutely,' I assured him. 'Thank you, Harold.' He nodded and went back to the growing crowd around the desk. I could see crew-cut there now, overcoat pulled up around his face. Behind him the man who had threatened to shoot me was watching me with dark suspicion. I tried to give him a smile of understanding, man to man, no hard feelings. He looked away.

The interview with Harold's psychiatrist friend, whom I'd never met before, took place in a bare room in the police station, just the two of us on either side of a table. He was around sixty with thinning hair, a tired face and heavy horn-rimmed glasses. The questions were routine: name, date and place of birth, parents' names, all of which I answered satisfactorily. Then he hit me with something I wasn't ready for. He asked me my home address.

I must have looked blank, because his eyes locked on to mine and he repeated the question. And suddenly I said, like it was the most natural thing in the world: 'Apartment 4b, Belvedere House, Castle Heights.'

How the hell did I know that?

The rest of the interview went like a dream – literally! Information poured out of me that I didn't know I had.

Even simple stuff like who was president of the United States came out as a name I'd never heard before, but it was the right answer. My social security number, which tripped off my tongue as though I knew it by heart, was absolutely new to me; and yet was, apparently, mine.

Slightly trickier was the question of what I had been doing in the garden of the house where I was arrested. However, I had realised that this would have to be explained, and I think I managed to turn it to advantage. I was trying to escape, I said, from what I considered to be an unjust incarceration in the hospital. Obviously my home was the first place they would look for me when I went missing – home, for this purpose, being the address I had given in the wealthy Castle Heights district. So, with what little money I had managed to steal, I had taken a taxi in the opposite direction. Fortunately Long Chimneys was more or less in the opposite direction, taking the hospital as starting point. I paid off the taxi, I said, intending to cover my trail by walking a while before finding another cab to take me to the station or the airport. However, I needed more money and was, frankly, hoping to steal some from the house where I was captured.

The shrink seemed satisfied with this explanation, then started to ask questions about Charlie. On this I was also ready for him and knew exactly what to say. I even managed to look embarrassed and give a kind of aw-shucks grin. I told him that I had been driving at the time of the accident and Anne was in the car with me. We'd been going to lunch across town with some people called Webber (never heard of them before!). I must have got a bang on the head, because when I came out of it I didn't know who or where I was. Nor did I now have any idea who Charlie was, even though I'd made a lot of noise about him at the time. 'Figment of the imagination, I guess. Hell, I don't know how the brain works. You tell me – you're the expert.' This was said with the same aw-shucks silly grin, with no hint of challenge or defiance in the voice. I knew that if I could just hang on to that pose and bury the truth along with my real feelings, then I was free and clear.

And I was right.

Anne came and sat with me for ten minutes while the shrink went to make his report. We held hands like a couple of lovesick kids in trouble for staying out late and waiting to hear the verdict of their elders, but we didn't say much. I think she was afraid to talk in case she triggered some response that might unbalance me again; and I know I was afraid to talk in case I told her the truth. I told her I loved her – that was the truth. She said she loved me and that everything was going to be all right. I said sure it was and she mustn't worry. It was good to see her relax a little.

Harold came in with a senior police officer – who looked afraid I might produce a razor out of nowhere and slit his throat – and said everything was arranged. The senior police officer, glad to see the back of us, ordered a car to take us home.

As we approached Castle Heights, with its imposing houses on both sides of the road, my life unfolded for me like a visit to some childhood haunt, where everything is the same, exactly as you remember it, only it's different. And the difference is in you.

We took the elevator up to 4b. Anne unlocked the door with its heavy carved panelling that I knew at once I'd never liked and never would, and the three of us went in. I tried not to make a performance out of looking around – the designer furniture carefully arranged around the large drawing room, the modern art collection on the walls, the soft rugs under foot. I was glad when Harold reminded me that the police driver was waiting downstairs to take back the stolen clothes that I was still wearing.

Without any hesitation I headed straight for the bed-room, found the switch that turned on the artfully placed lighting that illuminated an entirely art-deco bedroom and vast adjoining bathroom, and started to undress. The only shock came when I glimpsed my naked body in the mirror. I'm kind of ashamed to admit this, but it jolted me to see that I had no muscles. This was not the body of Rick Hamilton, who worked out rigorously in the gym three times a week. These shoulders slumped forwards lazily, and the stomach was beginning to rival the chest in girth. This was the body of Richard A. Hamilton – and he was flabby.

Even that revelation lost its edge as soon as it had registered in my brain. It was a long, long time since I, this 'I', Richard, had taken exercise. I pulled on a robe that hung in my closet, a black and red affair of silk from . . . India. In fact, as I continued to recall, from Delhi. Yes, that was it. I clearly remembered having been with Anne to India and staying with friends – whose name would later come to me – in Delhi.

I handed the stolen clothes, wrapped in a Nieman Marcus shopping bag, to Harold. Anne had made some tea and brought it in from the kitchen, but Harold said he ought to leave and headed for the door. I watched out of the corner of my eye as they conferred briefly in the hall. She seemed to be assuring him that everything was all right. He scribbled something on a piece of paper that he left on the small Chinese table by the door, called out goodnight to me, and left.

Anne came up behind the sofa where I was sitting, leaned down and put her arms around me, and held me like that for a while, her cheek pressing on the top of my head. We were, if I can put it this way, the same couple that we'd always been. We didn't need to say much. We often did – talk, I mean – but we didn't always need to. The closeness was there, unchanged.

Yet that night there was a loneliness in the room, an emptiness, something missing. Maybe it was only because of what I knew and that I couldn't bring myself to speak of. Or maybe it was always there, between this Anne and this me.

We drank some tea and went to bed. It was after one in the morning and she was as tired as I was, if not more so. She asked if I wanted something to help me sleep, but I said no. I tossed aside the silk pajamas that lay on my pillow, and she did the same with her night-dress. We climbed into the huge bed, turned off the lights, and rolled naked into one another's arms. It was then that she began to talk, that little whispering voice of intimacy and complete trust that I knew so well.

I don't remember what was said, soft words of love and reassurance, little private silly things. But I do remember her saying, 'Darling, don't ever frighten me like that again. I don't think I could live through it another time.'

Tenderness, longing and physical arousal rose up in me and ignited the same feelings in her. Exhausted or not, we made love with a gutsy luxuriousness that would have drained us both at even the best of times. But we needed this affirmation. I, I suppose, more than she, needed physical, tangible proof of a closeness that would never, whatever happened, let me down.

I must have slept for two, three hours. I looked at the clock when I woke and it was after four. Anne was sleeping, breathing gently, but I was suddenly restless and afraid to wake her. Not just afraid to wake her; I was more generally afraid, and I didn't know of what.

Yes I did. It wasn't any nightmare, any guilty secret; I felt no guilt. It was an overwhelming, agonising loneliness. Our lovemaking had only served to emphasise the impossibility of living with this great lie that had come between us. Suddenly I knew with utter certainty that I could not do it. I had to share with Anne the truth of what had happened.

More than that, I had to trust her to believe me. Without that trust I didn't want to live.

She stirred, as though responding to my thoughts.

'I have to talk to you.'

'What is it?' She pushed herself up on an elbow, anxious, suddenly alert, reaching for the light.

'Don't!' I put a hand on her arm. What I had to say to her I preferred to say in the same intimate darkness we had shared earlier. 'I know how this is going to sound, but I have to trust you, because you're the only person I can. So I have to. Try to understand.'

'Of course I do. Go on. What is it, darling? What d'you want to tell me?'

'It's, I . . . I'm not sure how . . . ' I was stumbling already. How to begin? I took a deep breath, wound up my courage, and plunged in. 'Darling, don't be alarmed by what I'm going to say. Above all, you must believe that I'm not crazy. What I'm going to tell you is the absolute literal truth, I'm making none of it up. Now I know how it's going to sound at first, but please just bear with me. I have some ideas about what's happened and how, but we'll get to that later. The most important thing you have to believe is that it changes nothing between us. The reason I'm telling you all this is because I love you. You're the only one I can really trust, and if I can't share this with you, then my life isn't worth living.' With that, I embarked on the whole story, right up to the actual moment of its telling.

When I'd finished Anne remained motionless and totally silent. She was lying on her pillow looking up at the ceiling. I could just make out the contours of her face as the first hint of pre-dawn light began to edge around the heavy curtains. Suddenly I saw what looked like a tear running down the whole side of her face, and I was seized by momentary panic. 'You do believe me, don't you?' In the course of recounting the events of the last few days I had re-lived them so vividly – especially the unbearable moment of her death – that it seemed impossible to me that anyone might doubt my word.

'Oh, my darling, of course I believe you!' She sat up and reached out for me, cradling and stroking my head against the softness of her neck and shoulder. 'Of course I do. You were right to trust me. What a terrible thing to have gone through alone, with nobody to turn to. But it's all right now, we'll cope with this together. You'll see, everything will be all right.'

The sense of relief that flooded through me as I heard these words was indescribable. I was lost in an alien, or nearly alien, world; two persons in one, with no control over what was going to happen next, or even what was going to flash into my mind; and yet I felt relief. I had the trust of the one person who could be my anchor and support in the face of whatever storms were yet to come. Relief turned into waves of irresistible exhaustion. I fell asleep right there, being held and stroked and comforted like a baby.

When I woke I was alone in the bed. The clock showed 8:45, and a strip of light around the still-curtained window suggested that the day was bright and sunny. I got up feeling better than I had in some time and pulled back the curtains. Yes, I recognised that view. I was like a man emerging from a long dark tunnel of amnesia. Except this tunnel had two ends, two separate and quite distinct realities, connected by a mystery that I must now begin to unravel.

First, however, I was hungry. I pulled on my robe and started for the kitchen, expecting to find Anne preparing breakfast. But as I opened the bedroom door I heard her talking to someone, and hesitated.

Then I realised that hers was the only voice. She was talking on the telephone. And she was sobbing as she spoke as though her heart was breaking. Which it was.

She was saying that she'd done her best, but she couldn't handle the situation any longer. They would have to come and take me away.

3

BY THE TIME the doorbell rang I was dressed and had almost finished packing an overnight bag that I had found in the bottom of my wardrobe. I hadn't made any sound to let Anne know that I'd overheard her phone call. I didn't blame her for it; she had merely reacted in the way any normal, caring person would. The fault was mine for having burdened her with something that for the time being, I now realised, I should have kept to myself.

Above all I was grateful that she hadn't returned to the bedroom where, I suppose, she thought I was still sleeping. I didn't want her to have to face me in the knowledge of what she had done. I didn't want her to lie to me, or I to her.

After I'd closed the bedroom door as she hung up the phone I had rapidly reviewed my options. Flight was pointless: how far would I get and what would it achieve? The best thing, I saw at once, was to stay and accept as equably as I could what was going to happen. I must show them by my behaviour that I was sane. Even if I had to submit to further tests and examinations, I reasoned, they would conclude that I was not unbalanced in any clinical sense. I would be released and I would persuade Anne – and anyone else I had to – to take my fantastic story seriously.

I was relieved that it was Harold who came into the bedroom and not Anne. He looked surprised to see me dressed and ready. 'Are you going somewhere, old buddy?' he asked, doing his best to sound cheery and casual. I smiled, hoping to reassure him that I was responsible and in control, and that he could trust me.

'It's all right,' I said, 'I know what's going on. I heard Anne on the phone. Thanks for being here, Harold – I wouldn't want her to have to deal with this by herself.'

'Look, Richard,' he said, obviously feeling acutely awkward, 'it's going to be all right, I promise you.'

'I know,' I said. 'Is Anne still here?'

He shook his head. 'I made her go across the hall to Irene Granger's place.' I remembered Irene Granger: a tall redhead, in her fifties and still great-looking, an ex-model divorced from a wealthy accountant. It was funny how I only had to hear a name now or see something in this other life and the memory of it slipped instantly into place. 'That's good,' I said, 'I'm glad you did that. Tell her she did the right thing. Tell her I don't blame her.'

He nodded. 'Sure.' Another awkward pause. 'Well – '

'I'm ready,' I said, snapping shut my overnight case.

'You won't need that,' he said.

'Might as well take it now I've packed it,' I answered, shrugging a question mark at the end.

'Okay. But we can send over for anything else you need.'

'I hope it won't be that long,' I said, trying to keep an edge of anxiety out of my voice. Stay relaxed, I told myself. Just stay relaxed.

'Of course not,' he responded – too quickly, I thought.

'By the way, where are we going? Not that last place, I hope.'

'No, no. I've made arrangements. They have the very best of . . . everything.'

Two men appeared in the door behind him. They were clean cut, well built, and wore ties and sports jackets. They could have been hockey players travelling to a match somewhere. They responded politely to my greeting but didn't smile. Downstairs one of them held open the rear door of a solidly comfortable station wagon. I turned to Harold: 'Aren't you coming with us?'

43

'I've got my own car,' he said, 'I'll go on ahead.' He unlocked the door of a shiny BMW. I smiled faintly, reassured that Harold still drove the same kind of car, although a different model from the one I was used to. I thought about suggesting that I ride with him, but didn't want to cause problems. I glanced up at Irene Granger's windows, saw a curtain move, then I got into the station wagon. One of the hockey players went around and got in alongside me. The other slid behind the wheel. He pressed a catch and I heard the doors lock. I made no comment.

The journey passed mostly in silence, my escorts making polite but monosyllabic responses to any effort I made to open up a conversation. About forty minutes out of town we reached tall iron gates which opened automatically and a security guard waved us through. At the end of a long gravel drive sat an imposing country mansion. Harold's car was already there.

The entrance hall was imposingly vaulted and pleasantly furnished. A nurse was climbing a curved staircase. Harold was waiting to greet me with his friend the shrink from the night before. 'You already know Dr Killanin,' he said. We shook hands and went into the doctor's spacious office. At one end, in the window, was a desk. At the other was a psychoanalyst's couch. The walls, where they were not covered by floor-to-ceiling bookshelves, were panelled in dark brown polished oak, with drab framed hunting prints hung here and there alongside various diplomas. The doctor sat behind his desk motioning me to sit opposite. Harold took a chair to one side, obviously intending to stay for this preliminary interview but not planning to participate.

Something about Killanin's voice made it strangely hard to concentrate on what he was saying, which was anyway fairly anodyne; but his sonorous, droning monotone deprived the words of meaning. This, I suddenly knew, was a man of no imagination or intellectual curiosity – certainly not a man capable of seeing my condition as anything more than a routine example of something he was already familiar with.

He was an administrator, a classifier, a man of received ideas: the very last man into whose hands I would have willingly delivered myself. I felt a momentary panic. Had I walked into a trap of my own making? Should I have run when I heard Anne on the telephone? The moment passed. I reassured myself that I had made the only possible decision.

I was suddenly aware that Harold was on his feet, preparing to leave. Killanin had risen, and so did I, feeling a twinge of alarm at the prospect of seeing my last lifeline to the outside world disappear. Harold must have seen something in my eyes because he looked puzzled briefly and anxious to get away. It was strange to feel so cut off from him. We should have been walking out of there together, cracking a joke, debating where to go for lunch; but instead he was leaving me there in that alien antiseptic atmosphere.

Without further ceremony Killanin handed me over to a senior nurse who would, he said, show me to my room. She had sharp, angular features which were emphasised by narrow, pointed glasses. She marched up the stairs with military precision, carrying my file under her arm like a rifle.

My room was large and airy with a broad bay window giving a commanding view of the grounds. It could have been a room in a country hotel except for being somewhat underfurnished. Conspicuously missing were telephone, television or radio; there was, however, a miniature television camera set into the wall above the door. The room contained no sharp edges, nor anything that could easily be broken to provide them. As in the hospital, the windows were obviously reinforced and had special catches to prevent their opening wide enough for escape. I thanked the nurse for showing me up and resisted the impulse to reach into my pocket for a tip; irony I felt would not have been appreciated.

Left alone, I wondered what was expected of me. Obviously I was under observation through the television camera. I wondered who was at the other end of it. Killanin? Somebody I hadn't yet met?

The adjoining bathroom, as in the hospital, was windowless. It was also without a trapdoor in the ceiling or any other possible means of escape. I looked around for another camera, and eventually saw it embedded in the centre of the ceiling. This was a level of intrusion I was not going to find easy to live with. However, I reminded myself of my purpose in going there willingly. It was to establish my sanity. That, and that alone, must be the focus of my attention.

An hour and a half later a different nurse entered and told me that Dr Killanin and a colleague were ready to see me. I had passed the time sitting by the window reading a paperback I had brought with me. Originally I had meant to bring *The Secret Agent* by Joseph Conrad. I had found it by my bed at the apartment and remembered starting it some time ago with pleasure. Also, to be quite honest, it had struck me as the sort of reading matter unlikely to make a bad impression; but then I had immediately checked the tendency towards becoming obsessed with the impression I was making as being in itself, at least to an unsympathetic observer, evidence of abnormality. So I had picked a book at random, which turned out to be somebody's account of a trip across Russia and was unutterably boring. However, I had dutifully plowed through several chapters with the intention of establishing for my televisual observers that I was perfectly capable of sustaining normal concentration.

I was taken back to Killanin's office. With him was a younger man with a fresh face, tightly curling blond hair, and a handshake that indicated such a need to be recognised as an honest 'good ol' boy' that I prayed he was someone whose opinion on my mental state would not be sought. My heart sank when Killanin introduced him as Dr Steve Sherwood.

Killanin conducted the discussion with the three of us seated in a triangle before the fireplace, in which there was an old-fashioned electric radiator of which only half was turned on. I was gratified at least that no mention had been made of employing the couch over by the wall.

I was by now becoming accustomed to psychiatric small-talk – those bland, introductory rondos by which they feel their way towards some tentative diagnosis. Frankly I took a certain pride in doing all I could to obstruct this process, since I felt there was no diagnosis to be made. However, I was reckoning without the fact that in the minds of my two interlocutors the diagnosis had already been made, and all they were seeking now was corroboration. Dr Sherwood was the first to challenge me directly with my 'other life' to which he understood, as he put it, I had recently referred. I smiled indulgently and told him that the things people said after getting bumped on the head should not, surely, be taken too seriously. He then asked me earnestly, leaning forward with his elbows on his knees and his fingers interlaced, why I had repeated the story to my wife during the night if I had, as I claimed, fully recovered from the mild concussion caused by my accident.

This required dealing with carefully. I knew that I was approaching a crucial border where I would either be declared sane and allowed to pass over into freedom, or labelled insane (or whatever euphemisms they chose to employ) and held, in effect, prisoner. I had to proceed with extreme caution.

'Look,' I began, 'if I tell you that I accept I was hallucinating, that what I said in the middle of the night was a result of a particularly vivid dream which revived, if only temporarily, that hallucination, then need we really go any further with this?'

They exchanged a look, reflected a moment, then Killanin took up the questioning. 'Put like that, no, I suppose not. But let's just for the sake of argument, and since we're here, let's just suppose that what you experienced was something more than hallucination. Could you offer any possible explanation for it?'

He was perhaps smarter, I decided, than I had initially

suspected. But it was the cleverness of an advocate determined to prove his case rather than that of a genuine seeker after truth. I was determined not to be drawn into his trap. 'No,' I said, 'I don't believe I could.'

'But we have been led to understand,' Killanin went on, 'that you indicated to your wife that you might have an explanation to this phenomenon, something you told her you would get around to talking about later, once you had convinced her of the reality of what had happened.'

I cursed myself again for having subjected Anne to such a seemingly preposterous story without more careful preparation. 'I suppose,' I said, 'that if you were to go into the wilder realms of the imagination, then you could probably cook up some kind of story to make sense of it.'

'Then why don't we do that?'

'No – you mean why don't *I* do it. And the reason I won't is because you will take such speculation on my part as proof positive of mental instability. And I am not in any way mentally unstable.'

'Aren't you afraid,' Sherwood put in, 'that we might just as well take your refusal as symptomatic of a paranoia which we might equally regard as, well, unusual?'

Checkmate, or almost. I stayed cool. 'That's a risk I am prepared to take,' I told him, attempting a smile to show that I was enjoying this intellectual cut and thrust between equals.

There was a pause. Killanin leant over to Sherwood and whispered something to which Sherwood nodded his agreement. Killanin then turned back to me. 'Mr Hamilton,' he began, dropping his gaze to the carpet for a moment, 'there is absolutely no question that you are a highly intelligent man fully in control of all your faculties. However, there is clearly something here which we, and surely you too, would very much like to get to the bottom of. I am proposing, therefore, that we inject you with a very small dose of – '

'No!' They both looked at me, impressed by the force of my refusal.

48

'Mr Hamilton,' Killanin started up again after a moment, 'the fact of your resistance to this course indicates quite clearly your feeling that you may not be as fully recovered as you would like to believe. Surely you must see that.'

It was becoming increasingly difficult to stay calm now, because I could see exactly where this was going. However, I made an effort and managed to keep my voice steady. 'No,' I said, 'I don't see anything of the sort.'

Another look was exchanged between them. 'Surely you must be aware,' Killanin continued, 'that we are in a position to insist on such a course if we think it is necessary in your best interests.'

I knew then that I had lost. Anger rose up in me, but I stamped on it. 'I think, if you don't mind, I would like to call my lawyer,' I said coldly, glancing towards a telephone on the desk. Killanin remained intransigent. When he spoke again there was a quiet though unmistakable threat behind his words. 'Mr Hamilton, papers have been signed and you have been committed to our care for your own good, and no other reason. We would be derelict in our duty if we allowed you to refuse or in any way obstruct the treatment which, in our professional judgment, you are in need of. I beg you to reflect on that very seriously, and cooperate.'

There was a silence. Both looked at me, and I looked back at them. 'You are making a very grave mistake,' I told them, 'and I must warn you that when I get out of here you will regret it.' I stood up. They must have read something aggressive into the gesture, because I saw in both of them a slight, though marked, instinctive recoil. 'I am now leaving,' I said, 'and I don't advise you to try and stop me.' It was foolish bravado, of course, though even now I cannot blame myself for giving way to it. After all, there is for any of us a limit to the amount of pushing around we will take from people whom we don't respect, and I suddenly, perhaps rashly, knew I had reached it. I started for the door.

'Mr Hamilton, please sit down.' It was Killanin. Both he and Sherwood were on their feet now. I ignored them and wrenched open the door, half expecting it to be locked, but it wasn't. Out of the corner of my eye I saw Killanin lunge towards his desk and press something. There was no immediate response, but before I was halfway across the hall the two hockey players who had brought me there appeared out of nowhere. They had discarded their ties and sports jackets and wore the white coats of male nurses now. With the awful calmness of professional thugs they seized my arms and pinned them behind me. One of them had his forearm across my neck and began to squeeze my windpipe in a choke-hold. I fought, I suppose I must admit, like a maniac. I screamed and raged and kicked, but they lifted me off the ground and carried me away with no more trouble than if I had been an angry, helpless child. I cursed them, I cursed Killanin, who was following, issuing instructions. I cursed Harold for letting this happen to me. I cursed, God forgive me, Anne.

But above all I cursed myself for having been such a fool. For having thought I could outwit the forces I was up against. For having thought that I could pick my way through this minefield of obstacles using only reason and good sense. It hadn't worked.

I was going to have to find another way.

It was dusk when I woke. I was in my room but strapped to the bed in a half sitting-up position. Drowsiness did not abate my anger and I refused to eat or swallow the now familiar little plastic cup of pills that was pushed under my nose. They rigged up a drip-feed and fed whatever they wanted direct into a vein.

The rest remains in my memory as a blur of more injections, questions, tests, and streams of bitter, bilious invective pouring out of me with a force that defied my physical exhaustion. The dam had broken and I came apart. It was like grief held in too long. The two selves within me, relieved of the strain of keeping up appearances, went to war with one another and with everything around them. I was I think, for a time, truly insane. The irony is that during this 'insanity' I told my story time and again, sometimes in more detail, sometimes in less; sometimes weeping, sometimes screaming, sometimes with quiet weariness. I told the simple truth. And for that I was kept strapped like a dangerous maniac to my bed, manhandled humiliatingly on to bedpans by the hockey players, held in their vice-like grip to be washed and have my incipient bed-sores treated by one of a rotating group of faceless nurses. Every demand to see my wife, my lawyer, or anyone else, was refused with the chilling finality of people who enjoyed total power over me.

A numbing, dull despair began to seep into my bones. I would have said into my soul if I'd thought I had one, but I didn't dare use words like that with their overtones of immortality, because that would have left me stranded and alone in that limbo for eternity. I would have been in hell. So I settled for a wretched, tortured here and now, in which I longed for death as my only escape.

Then Emma Todd returned. It was, I think, a morning, but I wasn't sure. Time meant little any more. I was trying to make it mean nothing – a defence mechanism, I suppose. I heard the tap of her cane as she found my bed. When I opened my eyes she was pulling up a chair. She smiled almost shyly in greeting, blind eyes staring across me at the wall.

'Hello, Rick. How are you?'

I'd lost the habit of being called Rick and it sounded strange. Then I remembered I'd told her to call me Rick at our first meeting. 'What are you doing here?' My voice, I realised, was dry and cracked. 'D'you work here?'

'No. But I was one of Dr Killanin's students ...' I gave a grunt and muttered something obscene. She went on quickly, obviously aware that we were being watched and listened to on television. 'I asked to be allowed to see you.'

I looked at her. 'Why?'

51

'Because I heard you were being difficult and I wondered why.'

'You heard *I* was being difficult!' I spluttered, trying to sit up.

Her smile broadened, as though she was teasing me. 'Don't get excited. I know how things must seem to you. Please believe me, you're not being tortured and nobody here is a sadist – I believe those are two of your favourite accusations.'

'When I get out of here that bastard's going to jail,' I growled. 'Either that or I'll kill him.'

She was unfazed by the threat. 'All right, but let's worry about that when you get out. That's what I'm here for – to get you out as soon as possible.'

Of course I didn't believe her. It was another trick. 'They haven't let anyone see me, not even my wife!' I could hear a whining tone in my voice that I didn't like. I sounded close to tears of self-pity. 'I want to see my wife, I want to see my lawyer, I'm going to sue this fucking establishment to Kingdom Come! They've kept me strapped down like a prisoner in some fucking mediaeval dungeon, they've used drugs on me like I'm some experimental fucking guinea-pig, they've – '

'Rick, Rick . . . I know how you feel, but calm down. Of course your wife has wanted to see you, but that might only have upset you more. She agreed that for the time being she wouldn't come. You've only been here four days.'

That came as a shock. 'Four days? You're lying. I must have been here for . . . '

'Four days. I can prove it if you like, or you can take my word.' I didn't answer. 'Dr Killanin knows perfectly well that nothing he's tried so far seems to have helped you. On the contrary, you've got worse. Now listen to me, Rick, none of the drugs that have been used on you have been in any way unusual. In fact the doses have been smaller than is normal. So whatever it is that hasn't been working – '

'Is my fault?' I snapped.

52

'No. It just means that we haven't understood the problem yet.'

I gave a cynical laugh. 'My dear Dr Todd, if you understood the problem, you'd be as crazy as I am – and probably strapped down in the next room.'

'Call me Emma.'

'Not while you're working for these bastards.'

'Rick . . .'

'Piss off!'

She sighed audibly. I felt a momentary rush of satisfaction; I had made a shrink sigh. Then immediately I thought: this is pettiness beyond all reason, I'm becoming as crazy as they think I am. 'Sorry,' I mumbled, ashamed.

'Have you ever been hypnotised?'

I looked at her, taken by surprise. 'No.'

'Would you be willing to try it?'

'D'you mean I have a choice? I haven't had a choice about much else in here.'

She smiled again, acknowledging my complaint, indulging me. 'It isn't possible to hypnotise anybody against their will, so it's entirely up to you whether we try it or not. As a matter of fact, some people can't be hypnotised at all, no matter how willing they are. If you're one of those, then the whole question's academic. But I'd like to try.'

'You?'

'I know what you're thinking. How can a blind person hypnotise you? You're thinking about somebody waving their hands and staring into your eyes, but that's just stage magic. It doesn't work like that at all. As a matter of fact, hypnotism's kind of a specialty of mine.'

'How do you do it?'

'I light a candle and have you look at it while I talk to you. That's all.'

'And that's enough?'

'If it's going to work at all, yes.'

I thought this over. 'How would you know I wasn't faking?'

'I'd know.'

I thought it over some more. I couldn't deny I was curious. 'All right,' I said.

Under Emma's instructions the nurse partially closed the curtains – enough to ensure that the daylight didn't drown the flickering candle that she then had the nurse light and place on a tray across my bed. I had been freed of my restraining sheet and fresh pillows were put behind me. The nurse then went to sit quietly in a corner and I forgot she was there.

'Just make yourself comfortable, relax, settle back, watch the flame . . . don't try to see anything in it, don't look for shapes, because that's your mind working, and I want you to empty your mind . . . just look into the flame, right into the heart of the flame, see if you can find the point where the flame begins, that little halo around the candle wick where the flame begins to burn . . . ' Her voice went on, saying nothing, just coaxing gentle, soothing rhythms from the air, while I sought and found the heart of the flame and gazed into it. 'You can see it, can't you, Rick? You can see it now, you see the heart of the flame . . . and the still, quiet centre at the heart of the flame . . . keep looking into it, Rick . . . deeper, deeper . . . into the centre of the centre . . . deeper, deeper, down and down . . . ' And so on and so on. I paraphrase, because I frankly don't remember too much of the detail. The experience was not disagreeable, in fact fairly pleasant and surprisingly restful after what I'd been through. But I didn't think anything was happening. I certainly didn't feel drowsy, but then I heard her telling me to close my eyes, and I obeyed instinctively. She then told me that all I would be aware of from now on was her voice. I would not want to open my eyes, I would not hear any other sound. And in that silence and that stillness I would speak with her.

After that, oblivion.

Until I heard: 'One, two, three.' I opened my eyes. I felt wonderful – refreshed, confident, a new man.

'How d'you feel, Richard?' she asked.

'I feel great. Wow! I don't know what you did, but it was worth it.'

'Tell me, Richard,' she said, 'who is Rick?'

For an instant my mind was a blank. I didn't know what she was talking about. Then the whole incredible story came flooding back. I felt embarrassed. I think I actually blushed. But I knew I had to answer – and I knew I had to tell the truth. 'Rick was just, I guess, a figment of my imagination. A kind of alternative version of myself.'

'You made him up?'

'Well . . . yeah, I guess so.' I gave a slight, self-conscious laugh, feeling acutely silly.

'And Charlie. Who was Charlie.'

'Oh, come on,' I said, starting to be really mortified by the absurdity of the whole thing. 'Gimme a break, will you? I mean I know I've been hallucinating, but that's all over now. Can't we just forget it and make a fresh start?'

I wasn't allowed home right away, of course. That would have been too much to expect. For one thing I was physically debilitated and in need of rest. The shots and pills they were giving me now were mostly vitamins, but the real reason for the swiftness of my progress towards recovery was psychological. I was at long last relieved of the terrible delusion that I was two people in one.

It would have been wrong to describe my former condition as schizophrenic. That is a loose, layman's use of the term. Schizophrenia is a very different, more generalised and less focused, form of the hallucinatory experience that I had been suffering from. Also schizophrenia arises largely, it now seems, from facts of body chemistry and less than was once thought from environmental influence. I don't think there are any instances of its having arisen, as my condition did, out of post-shock trauma. I learned a great deal after that first – the first of several – hypnosis session with Emma Todd.

One thing I learned from conversations not only with Emma but also with Dr Killanin and Steve Sherwood – both of whom I discovered to be charming individuals as well as front-rank, caring members of their profession – was the extraordinarily detailed nature of the hallucinations of which the human mind is capable. They told me stories and gave me books to read containing case histories of men and women who had imagined things far beyond the scope of my own rather limited 'alter ego'. One was the history of a young man, a scientist, who had fantasised that he was lord of a planet in an interplanetary empire in a distant universe. He was able to go there for weeks or months at a time, engage in the most complex political and military activities, then return to his life on earth and continue with whatever he had been doing – working at his desk, talking to a colleague, drinking a cup of coffee – as though he had suffered nothing more than a momentary loss of concentration. When he finally opened up about this secret 'other life' to an analyst, he was able to draw maps of incredible complexity and fill hundreds of pages with minute details of this distant civilisation. He even invented a whole language, together with historical notes about its origins and variations in other parts of the empire. It was fascinating, and I don't mind admitting that it made me feel a whole lot better about my own situation. He recovered, of course, as I was recovering; not in his case through hypnosis but through a lengthy and somewhat irregular form of analysis. But he returned successfully to normal life, after going through something which made my own inventions of a dead wife and non-existent child seem puny by comparison.

I was unexpectedly nervous before Anne's first visit to me in the clinic. One of the extraordinary things about delusion is the patient's utter certainty that he is right and the rest of the world wrong. Part of my mind had pushed Anne into this 'rest of the world' category. That she should feel hurt, rejected and distanced from me was only to be expected. I was worried about re-establishing the intimacy that we had always taken for granted between us. Was part of her from now on always going to feel alienated from me by the memory of this episode?

In the event I need not have worried. She had spoken with Emma, Steve Sherwood and Dr Killanin, and they had prepared her well. Her main concern, it turned out, was that I should not feel as though she had abandoned me during those awful first few days in the clinic when she – on their advice – did not visit me. Happily, I was able to reassure her on this point very quickly.

After her first visit Harold came to see me. 'Richard,' he began, his gaze grave, affectionate, solidly reliable, 'the most important thing is you get well. The business is under control, so don't let any of that weigh on your mind.' Indeed, quite honestly, I hadn't given business much thought. The real estate market was in one of its periodic downturns. Fortunately, being cautious by nature, I had seen it coming and adopted strategies to ride it out. The company was cash rich and over-leveraged properties had been unloaded, cutting debt to a minimum. In view of rising interest rates, that was a very comfortable position in which to find ourselves. Gail sent in some paperwork from the office, but there was nothing in it to cause me any concern.

Exactly three weeks to the day after my first hypnosis session I was signed out. Anne came to collect me in her new Jaguar, the customised maroon XJ6 that I had given her on her last birthday. I shook hands with all the staff who had been so kind and kissed goodbye to the nurses. We set off down the long gravel drive and were saluted through the gates by the security guard.

It was good to be back home. We both knew, though we hadn't said anything – we didn't need to – what was going to be the first thing on our agenda. More than once she had been tempted to climb into bed with me in my room at the clinic, but despite Roger Killanin's discreet assurances that the TV surveillance system had been switched off at central control, we both felt constrained by the presence of that staring eye embedded in the wall. Maybe to some couples it would have been a stimulus, but we weren't like that.

Anne closed the curtains of our bedroom against the afternoon light. We undressed quickly, rolled back the sheets, and made love.

But I'm still here.

Rick.

Yes, RICK!

Widower of Anne, father of Charlie. Poor little Charlie, where is he? I should be with him, instead of trapped inside the mind (if that's the word) of this spineless, dumb, near-doppelganger of myself who's making love to the equally near-doppelganger of my dead wife. He's inside her and I'm inside him. Boy, wouldn't that just freak the both of them if they knew!

(I'm sorry if that last remark was a little vulgar, but you're liable to get a little vulgar when you're mad – in the sense of angry, that is.)

Ever since that first hypnosis session it has been clear to me that there isn't room for the two of us in this world, unless we both want to live under lock and key indefinitely. I don't know about him, but I certainly don't.

Actually, that's not true, I do know about him, only too well. I'm getting to know more all the time. He couldn't take it again. He'd crack up totally next time. The guy's got no inner resources whatsoever: he's a real estate developer, for Chrissakes! So it's up to me to see that there isn't a next time. I must lie low, hiding in the folds of his brain – a fugitive! It's not an ideal situation. In fact it's humiliating and stultifying, but when it's a question of survival you have to do whatever's necessary. Right now I have no choice but to stay very, very hidden. Hidden from the world in general, but especially from Richard A. (for Arthur, same as me, though I never use it) fucking Hamilton – pompous self-satisfied ass-hole! How I loathe that man! I am ashamed that I, Rick Hamilton, could be so closely related in the great scheme of universal parallels (to coin a phrase) to such a piece of shit! And what in God's name a woman like Anne – even though this Anne is not *my* Anne, she's still close enough – is doing married to such a man is beyond me!

Incidentally, one of the few good things about hiding in this guy's brain the way I am is that at least I've got my clarity of thought back. I mean now that I know that he and I are two wholly separate entities, and especially now that he thinks I've gone away, I don't have to do battle with his thoughts the whole time. I can *read* his thoughts without any trouble. I can roam pretty much anywhere I like in his mind and find out exactly what he's thinking (which isn't a lot), and he doesn't know I'm there!

(Actually, if I may continue this digression for a moment, that's an interesting point. I can read his *thoughts*, but I have a little more trouble with his *feelings*. I can, if you like, *read* his feelings, but I'm not altogether sure if I can *feel* them. I'm in his head – more accurately, in his *mind* – but I don't have any contact with his body. I don't mean to get into the whole mind/body debate; I merely observe that the nearest I can get to his actual *feelings* – either physically based such as pleasure and pain, or abstractions such as happiness or misery – is to note from the functions of his brain that he is feeling them. But I cannot get any closer to them than that.)

Anyway, back to that first hypnotic trance. It's important that you understand what happened. I had to play my cards very carefully. I wasn't sure to begin with whether I had an ally in Emma Todd or not. Something about her convinced me that she had a deep intuitive understanding of my situation. I felt that there was, if you like, some sort of special bond between us. Maybe she didn't fully understand in every detail what was happening with me, but she was at least capable of getting it if it was explained to her – unlike that sadistic bastard Killanin and his third-rate sidekick Sherwood. Maybe it was to do with her blindness, I don't know, but right from the start there was an intensity to the way she listened. You knew that you had her attention. But under hypnosis ... Wow!

However, let me take things one at a time. You will remember that Emma, when she came into my room at the clinic, addressed me as Rick. This was because I had told her to call me Rick back in the hospital where we first met. However, by the time she came to visit me in the clinic, I knew that I was living, at least outwardly, the life of this other person, Richard A. Hamilton. So all the time she was saying 'Rick', I was kind of unconsciously letting it go right past me, Rick – with the result that *he*, *Richard*, was the one who was actually getting hypnotised, not *me*!

At least that's how I think it was working. Maybe I'm one of those people who, like she said, are immune to hypnosis, while Richard is a natural subject. I don't know about that yet. Maybe that's something I'll find out later.

Meanwhile, Richard ('Rick' to her) went out cold, and I, the real Rick, had the field to myself. The feeling of liberation was incredible! I got a whole new perspective on my problem. I realised immediately that the only reason I was in this mess, this immediate mess, kept prisoner in the clinic, was that he and I – that is Richard and I – had been battling for possession of the same ground: the so-called mind of Richard A. Hamilton, real estate developer.

Suddenly, looking back, I saw it all. One moment I was kneeling by my dying Anne, and the next I had flipped (again, I'll get around to how later) into this other version of myself who was also holding his wife's hand at the scene of an accident, but not the same accident and in not quite the same circumstances.

To begin with, of course, I didn't know where I was. How could I? But, equally important he, Richard, didn't know what had happened to him. I came on, as it were, so strongly that I almost knocked him right out of his own ball park for a while. At least he was so stunned that he just lay down and stayed quiet; while I, as you will remember, began to look around and ask myself what the hell was going on.

There I was, suddenly living someone else's life; and that someone else was in many ways (though not, thank God, all ways) a clone of myself.

The problems started when *he* began to recover from the initial shock of my arrival – or, from his point of view, invasion. To me it seemed like I was beginning to remember things I didn't know I knew. What was actually going on was that he, Richard, was beginning to come to and attempt to re-possess himself. It was a state of affairs that couldn't have continued, and didn't. When I look back now, it was all clearly inevitable: my 'confession' to Anne; her perfectly normal reaction (though I'm still not convinced that 'my' Anne would have done the same thing); his – Richard's – fear and panic on finding himself locked up like a lunatic; and my rage and despair at finding myself chained to this lunatic and condemned to share his fate. We couldn't function together. It was simply impossible.

So there I was in this hypnotic trance with Emma. I couldn't see her of course because he, Richard, had his eyes closed – and his eyes were all I had. But the closeness between us in that wonderful, serene atmosphere of the trance was, well, almost ecstatic.

'Rick?' she began. 'Can you hear me, Rick?'

'Oh, my God, can I hear you!' I replied. 'I can't tell you how wonderful it is to hear you. I mean, you really know I'm here, don't you? I wasn't sure that you did, but now I know you do.'

'I know you're there,' she said, her voice gentle, soothing, caressing. 'I want to talk to you. I want you to tell me about yourself.'

So I told my story yet again, but better than I'd ever told it before. I even began to approach an explanation, or at least a theory, of what had happened. I admitted that I wasn't a trained physicist, but I told her about the *Particle/Wave* magazine I published in my other – my *real* – life which gave me at least a general grasp of what was going on at the frontiers of the subject. I told her that she could verify everything I was about to say in one conversation with any university physics professor, which surely wouldn't be too much to ask.

Then, abruptly, I stopped. Something was wrong. I felt suddenly that I was going too far too fast. I sensed a warning coming from her. Being right, I realised, was not enough. It was certainly no defence against the charge of being insane! *Proving* you're right is all that counts in the blundering world of everyday commonsense reality; and I couldn't prove anything. Even Einstein, if he came back today, couldn't *prove* that space and time were curved. All he could do would be to show that nobody else had come up with a better idea that *disproved* his theory. (He would also, incidentally, have to admit that one of his notions, the EPR 'thought experiment' in 1935, had been totally invalidated by Alain Aspect's experiment in Paris in 1982. So, in the end, where are you?)

Anyway, I stopped right there (before I got on to the trickier theories about what *really* happens when an observer watches a quantum wave 'collapse' into a particle) and told Emma that I didn't want to discuss the matter any more. Respecting my decision and, I am sure, at least on some level understanding the motives behind it, she said okay and woke him – Richard – up.

He seemed quieter after that. They all noticed it. That's because *I* was quieter. As a result he was less aware of my presence. But I was thinking. I was planning what I must do. It was difficult, and he was aware of something going on and kept blurting out odd things that I had wanted to keep to myself. It was a nuisance, but I was increasingly confident that I could get around the problem in time.

The chance to perfect my strategy came in, and only in, those hypnosis sessions with Emma. I'd figured out what she was doing and I made the most of the opportunity she was offering me. She was giving me the time, the privacy, the freedom from *him*, to think. Those sessions with her, with him under hypnosis and sleeping like a fat, overfed dog in front of the fire, gave me time to get my thoughts together.

I realised, because she had told me, that our sessions were being recorded. And anyway I knew that the television up on the wall was watching and listening the whole time. So it was obvious to me that the last thing I should do was insist on the differences between myself and Richard. That would in itself be taken as sufficient evidence for keeping me – both of us – locked up here indefinitely. And Richard, being too dumb and scared to handle it, would just freak out like before and I wouldn't be able to control him. Clearly, it was up to me to take the initiative. And this, I realised, was what Emma was giving me the opportunity of doing.

And so, by the end of our fourth session of hypnosis, I did what the camera on the wall and the listening microphones wanted me to do: I played 'cured'. I, Rick, instead of repeatedly explaining who I was and how I came to be there, gradually allowed myself to fade, or appear to fade, like the smile of the Cheshire cat, into nothingness. Until suddenly I was no longer there at all.

My last card of the game, its playing, even if I say so myself, impeccably timed, was to say to Emma towards the end of that fourth session: 'Emma, why do you keep calling me Rick? My name's Richard. Everybody calls me Richard. It's not that I'm particularly fussy, but it just feels strange to be called Rick.'

There was a pause. I could feel her pleasure and, indeed, pride. She knew I had taken full advantage of the opportunity which she had given me. I knew then that I was home and dry. It was over. At least this part of it.

'All right, Richard,' I heard her say, 'now I'm going to wake you up. When I count to three you will wake up feeling relaxed, refreshed, and full of confidence. And "Rick" will have gone away completely. Now: one, two, three . . .'

And the slumbering moron woke up, and felt great. And I settled back, very quiet, knowing now that patience, secrecy and singleness of purpose were my best allies.

I can handle the situation, at least for the time being.

Long enough, I hope, to find the way out that I know is there somewhere. One thing I have to do is get control of *him* without his knowing it. Or if I can't do that, at least reach some kind of understanding whereby he won't obstruct me, and might even help me.

Because I can't do anything without him, I'm incorporeal. Without at least temporary use of his physical being I'll never get out of here.

And if I don't, if I finally do begin to feel that I am trapped indefinitely and fall into despair . . . then I really might become insane.

And I wouldn't like to be him if that happened.

4

WITH EVERY MINUTE spent in this man's company I despise him more. When he looks in a mirror I look away – not literally, of course, because I don't have eyes to look away with. But what I do is avoid contact with those parts of his brain that register, through his eyes, his reflection. And I especially avoid those areas of his brain that give a little tremor of self-satisfaction at what they see.

Oh, the pleasure I could have with this fool if I dared to turn the search-light of my scorn full blast on to his furtive inner self: the shabby secrets, shoddy thoughts, the narrow and self-serving aspirations that he passes off as honest ambi-tion. My God, is this what we're all like inside? Are we really taken in by the external charades we put on for each other? Or do we just pretend to believe each other's lies? And if so, why? Do we need companionship that badly?

I can't – *won't* – believe that that's all there is to this thing we call 'society'. There's got to be some hope, surely. Even the fact that I *want* there to be hope is itself a kind of hope. But my God, it's a pretty thin basis for optimism about the future of humanity.

I said it again: 'My God'. Am I becoming religious?

Are You there? Is anybody there?

Silence. What did I expect?

I expected silence.

No, I'm not becoming religious. I'm no more (and no less) religious than anybody else when faced with the gross, appar-ent meaninglessness of existence. Why, we ask ourselves, do we search for meaning if there is none? Where does the idea come from? The fact that we think of it means it must exist somewhere — bingo, God!

On the other hand, perhaps meaning isn't 'out there' to be found, but is something we create for ourselves. In that case does it have any meaning outside our need for it? Does our need give it meaning?

Search me.

Somebody once said that no man is a hero to his valet. I've never had, or been, a valet; but I can tell you with some authority that no man is a hero to anyone who knows what he's thinking.

Enough! What right do I have to this superior moral tone?

Just because I have this bird's (or worm's — birm's?) eye view of Richard A. Hamilton doesn't make me any better. I'm looking out of myself at the inside of him. How do I know there isn't somebody doing the same inside me, and feeling just as repelled? After all, Richard A. Hamilton *is* me, or a near enough facsimile to be embarrassing. Count your blessings, Rick: list the differences.

I've already mentioned one — he takes no exercise. I find that very hard to understand. How can anyone who's almost me be so unphysical? I'm not trying to imply I'm Mr Universe or anything, or that he's a slob with a gut hanging over his belt. He dresses carefully and, knowing he has a tendency to run to fat, he watches his weight more closely than I do. He actually lunches quite often in one of those restaurants where they give you a calorie count of your meal with your bill. I couldn't help letting out such a snort of derision the first time we went there that he almost heard me.

Secondly, he has no children and shows no interest in having any. All right, I can understand that people on the whole don't miss what they've never had. Nobody has an obligation to breed, in fact they're probably doing the world a favour by avoiding it. All the same it drives a wedge between us: I with the joy I found in parenthood, and he with the dull satisfaction he finds in playing the market and getting asked to the right parties.

Thirdly he has — are you ready for this? — political ambitions! Now listen, I won't deny I've thought about it. Be honest — who hasn't? At the very least you tell yourself you could do better than those fools on the Hill, in the Oval Office, the Governor's Mansion, wherever. And you probably could — if you went in there right now, today, as you are. But of course you can't. To get even a shot at the job you have to go through years of compromise and concession that leave you virtually undistinguishable by the time you get there from the people you're replacing.

This guy knows that, and it doesn't bother him. He accepts it. He actually has a game plan. You could call it half-baked or opportunistic, depending on how seriously you took him. It involves him making a lot of the right moves over the next few years and winding up as Governor. If it weren't for the fact that he was born outside of the United States, he'd be looking toward the Presidency. I can't believe this guy.

Actually I am the one fly in his ointment so far. The other day I listened in on a conversation between him and Harold that I was frankly hard pressed to believe. Harold is the one person in the world to whom he has confided these ambitions — apart from Anne, but he talks of them to her only in vague and general terms. But he and Harold are co-conspirators. Clearly Harold would be in line for a very senior post if things worked out.

The other day he sat down with Harold over lunch (at the calorie-counting place) and asked if in Harold's opinion his recent spell in the psychiatric clinic may have harmed his political prospects in the long term. Harold had obviously given the matter some thought already. His considered judgment was that probably no harm had been done. It wasn't as though Richard had been admitted for any actual illness. He hadn't suffered a breakdown or fallen prey to a depression that might raise questions about his fitness for high office. All that had happened was that he'd been in a car accident and suffered post-shock trauma brought on by a blow to the head. It wasn't exactly a plus factor, but the damage was controllable – especially if they managed to suppress the story of how he was found one night prowling around some strange house peering in the windows. If he were to become dubbed 'The Prowler' or, even worse, 'Peeping Tom' by his enemies, then the game would be up. But Harold was sure they could get over that problem by spreading a little money in the right places and getting a few signed undertakings from key witnesses.

Sometimes I worry about Harold – this Harold. I cannot believe that 'my' Harold would have taken such a cynically pragmatic view. Maybe lawyers just mirror the values of their clients.

But is that what friends do? I thought friends were supposed to tell you when you were talking bullshit, not just sit there nodding sagely and counting up their calorie intake. I thought Harold had standards.

And then there's Anne. What to say about Anne? Where to start? I've already mentioned the most obvious differences: the hair, the clothes. But there's also the body. It's the same body, it weighs the same, it goes in and out in the same places, but it's in better shape. Not that my Anne was in bad shape by any means. On the contrary! But my Anne didn't jog, didn't have an exercise bike in the bathroom, didn't go to the gym and work out with weights at seven in the morning. This one is, if I may put it so, more like me than I am.

All that is minor, however, by comparison with the differences I am now becoming daily more aware of. For one thing I see less of her than I used to. That is to say that she and Richard spend less time together than Anne and I did. She has a full calendar. When she's not organising a fund-raiser for the opera house she's doing it for the symphony orchestra, the art museum, or some hospital or university trust. Anne is into fashionable charities in a big way. I think, although I know she would hotly deny it, that she calculates the amount of effort she puts into a cause by the amount of cachet she expects to get out of it. I know it doesn't make her any different from most of the other women she sits on these committees with, but it's a terrible thing to say about someone you love.

Oh, yes, I still love her. I've tried not to. It would be easier if I didn't. I tell myself that she's a social-climbing phony married to an ambitious creep – and that's where my righteous indignation falls apart. Because it's all clearly his fault, and – I have to be honest about this – as there's something of me in him and something of him in me, I must accept my share of the responsibility for what he's made of her.

You may ask why, if Anne is still essentially and inwardly the woman I think she is, she doesn't simply rebel and refuse to play the role of rising social matron that he wants of her? Frankly, I don't know the answer to that, and it troubles me. Is this really the direction she wants her life to take? Could I, if I were Richard, have done this to *my* Anne? I find it hard to believe. My Anne has – had – more strength than that. My Anne would not have married this man. She would have laughed at his pretensions and gone her own way. Is it possible that the two Annes are as different as Rick and Richard?

How far I am from home.

I must hold on. I must not despair.

Their lovemaking is the hardest thing to live through. They're not as good together as we were, and that makes it worse. They have their routines. He knows what she likes, she knows what he likes. They don't talk about it, they don't ask each other questions the way we sometimes would. It's good sex, but ours was great. It's frequent, four, five times a week, but ours was more frequent. We never counted, it was just part of being together. Sometimes – this is the worst thing – he fantasises. He isn't making love to her at all but to some pornographic image in his mind. When we – my Anne and I – had fantasies we'd talk about them, play them out, enjoy them. His are sordid secret things. Sometimes he thinks about a woman that he's met or just glimpsed somewhere and her image takes the place of Anne. Other times he invents them. Does Anne do the same? I wonder.

One thing I know for certain: he doesn't chase after other women. I might respect him more if his reasons weren't so cowardly. Fundamentally he's too lazy. Also he's afraid of scandal. And disease. And there's a pragmatic streak in him which knows he'd be damn lucky to wind up with anyone better than Anne.

It's not good enough. It's unbearable. Here I am stuck in the recesses of his consciousness while he paws and grunts and sweats all over her. I feel like a voyeur, a sick pervert. When he has an orgasm, I don't. It happens in *his* body and *his* brain, not in *me* — whatever I am. All I'm aware of is the synaptic convulsion of his climax. It could as well be a sneeze as an orgasm for all it means to me. How I long to feel what his hands feel, to experience what his body is capable of offering, to mould and guide his movements to awaken in her the raw, real passion that I know is there — *must* be there. She isn't *my* Anne, but she's close enough. I love her and I want her. I could change her. I could make her mine.

But I can't.

Enough. Change the subject. Anything.

I must be clear and firm of purpose. My only hope is to find some way of communicating with him that will not set off the kind of panic that happened before. I could destroy him, and it would give me some satisfaction. But that would mean destroying myself too. It's a horrible dilemma. I must hold on.

What can I do?

Something awful has happened. It left me stunned, numb with shock, for half the day. But gradually I came to realise what I must do. It is my only chance.

Richard sleeps, I don't. Whatever it is that makes corporeal brains and bodies need those daily hours of oblivion doesn't affect me. While he sleeps I spend my time probing those regions of his mind that I'm afraid to enter while he's awake for fear of arousing his suspicions. Sometimes my movements trigger dreams in him, but dreams are acceptable. He knows about dreams. We all think we know about dreams. We take them for granted, however extraordinary, and push them aside when we wake. I've even tried talking to him in his dreams, hoping that maybe I could establish some kind of bridgehead between us. It didn't work. Part of him realised what was happening and the panic started up again. I had to stir up a quick smokescreen of all kinds of irrelevancies so that he passed the incident off as a standard nightmare.

I've combed back and back through his memory banks, comparing them with my own, noting where he made one decision where I had made another, or where things had happened to him slightly differently from the way they happened to me. The similarities between our lives are overwhelming, which makes the differences between us all the more extraordinary. I was just beginning to think that if the same was true of my Anne and this Anne, then there was hope yet that I might in time elbow this lumbering hulk of Richard aside and find a way to re-build between us, her and me, the relationship we had enjoyed in that other world. We might even – I don't know how these things work exactly, but our genes must be pretty much identical to what they were in that other world – we might even be able to have Charlie, or at least a child almost identical to him.

Then it happened, this terrible thing. It involved Anne.

Richard was due to fly to Chicago and stay overnight for a business meeting. His plane was in the early evening, but by mid-afternoon it was obvious that he was coming down with flu. He thought about calling Harold to have him go in his place, then remembered that Harold was in Phoenix working on an acquisition for another client.

So he cancelled his meeting, cancelled his flight, and went home.

Anne was out – probably, he thought, at one of her committees. He left a note for her just inside the door, swallowed some aspirin and vitamin C, and put himself to bed.

By the time she got back he was already half-asleep. I heard her come in, but he didn't. I heard her say something under her breath when she read his note and put her head into the bedroom. It sounded like she said 'Oh, no!', but very softly, barely a whisper.

She came closer and must have been standing over him for several moments before he sensed her presence and opened his eyes. She kissed and fussed over him and asked if she should call the doctor. He said absolutely not (he was a coward about doctors – more so than ever after having been shut up in that clinic). All he wanted, he said, was to sleep it off, maybe spend tomorrow in bed, then he would be fine. It was a twenty-four-hour thing that half the people in the office had already had. He apologised that probably she would catch it now and she told him not to worry about that, just get well. She said she'd let him sleep and look in later to see if there was anything he needed.

I've no idea how much later 'later' was. He was in a deep sleep by then and I was going over his memory of an important conversation that he'd had with his father when he was fourteen. I'd had the same conversation with my father – ostensibly about career possibilities, but really about what a man searches for in life – except for certain tiny details. I was trying to figure out if these details had ultimately led to some of the major differences between Richard and myself, when I heard the door open and Anne's footsteps come softly across the carpet.

His eyes were closed, so I couldn't see anything, but I could hear her breathing as she leant close. I supposed she just wanted to make sure that he was sleeping peacefully before going back to whatever she was doing. But just as she turned to leave the telephone rang.

To say it rang is an exaggeration. It had a soft tone which at the best of times would take some moments to penetrate even a light sleep. This was because Richard preferred to be coaxed awake rather than startled. On this occasion it barely even hinted at a first ring before – she was standing right by it – she picked it up.

She answered softly so as not to wake him, but as soon as she heard who it was she became flustered and afraid to talk. She needn't have worried. There wasn't even a flicker of response in Richard's brain. He was sleeping so heavily that a fire alarm wouldn't have roused him. Even I, fully awake, couldn't hear much – except that it was a man's voice at the other end.

'I can't talk,' she said in a muffled, urgent whisper as though her hand was shielding her mouth. 'He's here. I've been trying to call you. No, he didn't go, he's sick. I'm in the bedroom – wait.'

Very quietly she put down the phone, tiptoed out, closing the door with barely a sound, and presumably continued the conversation on a safe extension.

Richard slept on. But I . . . you can imagine how I felt. You can imagine how much I would have given for the use of his hands to pick up that phone and find out what was going on.

But I knew what was going on. There was no mistaking that tone of voice, that intimate conspiratorial guilt.

Anne was unfaithful.

Richard spent the next day in bed with a temperature, no appetite and a headache. Agnes the housekeeper stayed on a few hours extra to keep him supplied with mint tea, vitamins, and whatever else he needed during the day while Anne was out.

I, meanwhile, was near demented. Not only was the pain

73

of what I had discovered all but unbearable, but my impotence to do anything about it was driving me to distraction. I paced, metaphorically, back and forth in his brain for hour upon hour, wringing my hands and cudgelling my brains for an answer.

While he lay there like a sack of potatoes, sipping lemon-flavoured flu remedies, blowing his nose and blearily watching daytime television, I was being driven insane by lurid fantasies of where Anne might be, what she might be doing, and with whom.

In a sense, of course, it was none of my business. These people's lives were their own affair and I had no right to interfere. But, like all moral arguments, such a proposition had little or no place in the real world in which I found myself.

I was aware — how could I not be? — that the true source of my anguish was not what *this* Anne was doing, but what *my* Anne *might* have been capable of, might even have done, without my ever knowing. Could I have been living in a dream world, a fool's paradise all that time? Was — Heaven forgive me for the thought — was Charlie mine? There was no way now I could know anything for sure, but the more I could find out about *this* Anne in *this* life, the more chance I would have of understanding my own Anne in *our* life. I was fully aware that I might come up with some things about her which I had not previously suspected and which would be painful to confront. But I had no choice. I had to know.

And this passive, flu-ridden, steaming lump of lard had to find out for me. If that meant his finding out some painful truths for himself, so be it. I was ruthless in my desperation.

But how was I to make him do it? He suspected nothing. *Nothing!* It had never crossed his impossibly complacent mind that his wife might be unfaithful. To him their lives were on track and headed towards their pre-set goals. I wasn't even sure, when I came to think about it, how he'd take the news that he'd been cuckolded. Would he be devastated? Philosophical? Indifferent? Dangerous?

Supposing he committed suicide? Blew his brains out – and me with them.

I was facing a double problem: how to alert him to what was going on; and how to exercise at least some control over his response.

And suddenly – Eureka – I saw that I had stumbled on the answer to all my problems at once. Even before the shock of Anne's betrayal I had been searching for a way to communicate with Richard without throwing him once more into panic and confusion. Now I had it. I had the means not only to open a dialogue but also, I was fairly sure, to influence his behaviour. I saw now how I could make him accept me as a natural part of himself that must be listened to, not some alien invader to be fled from and resisted.

I would be the Voice of Jealousy.

The whole plan unfolded in my mind with an appalling simplicity. After all, it doesn't take a rocket scientist to figure out that a voice in your head saying 'I am your alter ego from another universe' is not necessarily to be trusted, and you may be wise to avoid operating heavy machinery until it goes away.

But the still, small voice of jealousy, that worm of doubt eating away at the back of your brain, that is a voice with a name to it, a voice you know about. Listening to that voice does not necessarily mean you are going crazy. Cloaked in that universal metaphor, I could step forward with confidence to centre stage and make my presence known at last.

Being feverish, Richard was in a particularly vulnerable state of mind. It seemed natural that thoughts should float into his consciousness from heaven knows where, trailing with them strings of free association leading to destinations as unknown as their origins. His resistance was low, he was suggestible. He thought he could indulge himself in fantasy and discard it when it suited him. He was wrong. This thought, my thought, once planted would not go away.

Within an hour I had convinced him that he, not I, had

overheard that snatch of conversation between Anne and her lover on the telephone. He couldn't be sure whether he'd dreamed it, or whether it had actually happened while he was half-awake. That doubt would not let go of him. I had him.

Towards the end of the afternoon Harold, back from Phoenix, called to ask how he was. He'd heard from Richard's secretary that he was ill and wanted to know if there was anything he could do. Richard almost asked him to come over right then so that he could pour out his wretchedness to the one man he had always trusted. At least Harold would know the name of a discreet private investigator should he need one. But he checked himself and merely mumbled rheumily that he expected to be over the worst by tomorrow.

Would that were true.

Anne seemed unaware of the suspicion in his eyes when she arrived home. She had a sparkle and a glow about her that deepened his depression into a despair. He tossed two effervescent vitamin Cs listlessly into a glass of water and stirred them with a pencil, which Anne took from him, saying that he'd get lead poisoning. She was telling him about her day, but he couldn't bring himself to listen. Too much of it might be lies, and he still couldn't bear to let her lie to him.

That night Anne, at his insistence, slept in the guest room because his wheezing and his coughing and his endless turning would only have kept them both awake. He couldn't face a night-long, sleepless silence between them.

I used the long dark hours to good advantage, filling his fitful sleep with graphic dreams of Anne in strangers' arms (culled from my memories of her times in mine), and his waking hours with the taunting voice of sexual self (or so he thought) mockery at his own inadequacies. The process afforded me no pleasure, but the situation offered no alternative.

By morning Richard A. Hamilton was my surrogate.

As predicted, the worst of the flu was over in twenty-four

hours. Richard, however, instead of rushing back to the office as he had intended, decided to spend another day at home to recuperate fully. At least that was the story he told Anne. He also told Agnes that she needn't stay on any later than usual, he would be quite all right alone.

He spent the afternoon in a frantic search for incriminating evidence of Anne's secret life. The backs of shelves, the bottoms of wardrobes, the deepest recesses of her clothes closet, purses, luggage, pockets, bedside tables, bathroom cabinets and kitchen drawers. Nothing. My ingenuity was running out, as his had long since. Only my insistence kept him going. But he was beginning to resist. He wanted to believe he was mistaken, that his suspicions were no more than the product of a flu-ridden, feverish imagination. He was trying to turn his back on the awful doubts that had beset him.

But that, of course, was an impossibility. We can no more ignore doubt than we can pretend we feel no guilt or superstitious fear. It is one of those plants that flourishes without our help, mocking our attempts to stifle, poison, starve, or cut it down. Richard knew that the failure of his search proved nothing – except, perhaps, the carefulness with which she was conducting her affair.

Or affairs, plural. Oh, yes, yes, yes, I still had him by the nose, his bid for freedom swiftly curtailed by the nagging Voice of Jealousy that threatened to follow him wherever he ran.

The next plan was surveillance. If we followed her for, say, a week or two and found her behaviour irreproachable, then even I might be willing to reinterpret what I had heard of that phone call in a more favourable light. Of course I didn't believe for a minute that this would be the case, but the assurance helped Richard get over his scruples about stooping so low as to spy on his wife.

One thing I was determined he should not do was hire an investigator. If I was to maintain and strengthen my hold over him, the last thing I needed was an outside confidant entering his life. I was already doing my best to dissuade him from talking to Harold – on the grounds that he would look a fool if his suspicions did in fact prove to be unfounded. Only if I had him to myself could I achieve what I needed to achieve.

So Richard took to playing detective. He had a dismally feeble imagination, but again I was able to prod him towards some kind of organised plan. Obviously it was impossible single-handedly to mount a twenty-four-hour-a-day surveillance, even though, anyway, at least twelve of those hours were spent in our company. The trick lay in divining through casual conversation, along with the odd furtive dip into her calendar, where she was going to be at different times of day – those endless meetings and committees, workouts and luncheons which were the fabric of her life. Then a phone call to leave a casual message, a drink with an acquaintance who had also been there, a suggestion that he pick her up for dinner at such and such a time and such and such a place – all these little strategies, put together, made it inevitable that very soon any lies she tried to get away with would begin to stand out like fingerprints on glass.

During all this time – about ten days – I was surprised by how well Richard withstood the inevitable stress and strain involved. To say that I felt a hint of admiration for him would be going too far, but I began to suspect that my previous scorn for his lack of moral courage may have been fractionally exaggerated. Outwardly he appeared utterly untroubled. Anne, I am sure, suspected nothing. When they made love – which they did three times during the period in question – he performed faultlessly and, if anything, with slightly more enthusiasm than normal. Only I knew that he had stepped into a porno theatre the previous Thursday and was re-living the main feature with gusto.

In the end, however, the turning-point came with surprising speed. He was just beginning to suspect that this whole thing had been a storm about nothing (and, to be honest, so was I; I was beginning to wonder what new disguise I could adopt after the Voice of Jealousy had been finally and firmly set aside) when all the little red flags that I had planted in his head stood on their ends and quivered.

Nine days earlier Anne had made a strange mark in her diary: 'B.M.', with a line running through the whole of Tuesday afternoon. Normally she wrote down enough to make clear what she was referring to – this committee or that friend, or such and such a restaurant or somebody's house. But 'B.M.' stood unqualified and cryptic in its isolation. Casually over dinner one night he had led the conversation by circuitous routes around to that particular afternoon, and had divined that she had lately been elected to a special steering committee for the forthcoming charity ball in aid of the City War Museum – a great honour, for which he expressed his approval. Naturally he didn't ask what relevance 'B.M.' had to the event, since this would have meant admitting that he had pried into her calendar.

But when the same 'B.M.' appeared again two days later, with yet another line scratched through the afternoon, he knew now that he must verify her story.

This time, in response to his subtle, cautious questioning, she said that she had spent the afternoon with her friend Valerie looking at collections of fall fashions. He didn't know Valerie well enough to call up and check, but he didn't need to. The inconsistency was proof enough. The iron fist of jealousy tightened its grip, and he prepared himself for a final confrontation with the truth.

It came the following Monday. 'B.M.' once more made its appearance in the calendar, accompanied as ever by the firm line announcing the exclusive, all-embracing nature of the rendezvous.

He asked no questions, carefully said nothing to indicate his suspicions . . . and followed her in a rented car, wearing dark glasses and with a hat pulled low over his brow.

Balthazar's Motel was at the upper end of the scale of those establishments advertising X-rated movies and waterbeds. The word 'Adult' winked knowingly in pink neon outside the manager's office.

From his vantage point in the parking lot of the 7-11 across the way, he saw that she had no need of management's assistance in securing a room. She had her own key in her purse and went directly to the door of, he discerned through his binoculars, cabin number nine.

It was, as he had feared, as unlikely a location for a meeting of the steering committee for the War Museum Charity Ball as for a showing of even the most immodest collection of fall fashions.

He waited, his heart palpitating and his breathing shallow, his camera with its long-range lens at the ready on the seat beside him.

Five minutes and forty-eight seconds later another car drew up and parked a few spaces away from Anne's. He recognised the shiny BMW at once. He clutched for a split second at the one last straw of hope: that Harold had lent his car to a colleague or a friend and knew nothing of the perfidious use to which it was being put.

But no. The driver was Harold himself. He got out, locked the vehicle, and went straight, eagerly even, to the door of number nine, and entered without knocking.

5

'STOP! NO! FOR God's sake don't!' I was shouting at the top
of my voice. *My* voice this time, no disguises. He knew
who I was. He realised I was back. He knew what was
going on. But he was beyond my control.

It was the thing I had most feared. I knew the danger
point would come when he faced the truth about his wife,
but I had felt confident I would be able to take over and steer
him the way I wanted him to go. What I had not bargained
for was Harold's appearance in the list of players.

Perhaps because I was myself as appalled by the discovery
as Richard was, I let my grip slacken for a vital moment. The
next thing I knew I felt like a novice rider whose horse has
bolted under him. I was shocked by the force of the sheer
blind fury that tore through him like a blood-red tidal wave,
levelling everything in its path – including me. By the time
I had gathered my wits and taken stock of the situation, he
was out of the car and striding across the road with a heavy
steel wrench in his fist.

'Don't do it! You'll only make it worse!'

'Shut the fuck up!' he bellowed. Pedestrians on the far
side looked over anxiously at the ferocious-looking man
coming towards them and apparently shouting at nobody.
They moved a little faster to get out of his way.

'Richard, you know who I am! I'm your friend! Trust
me!'

'Fuck you!'

A couple of passers-by broke into a run.

'Listen, this is the wrong way to handle it. You're going to lose! Do you want to be a loser?'

'I'll kill him! I'll kill them both!'

'Then what?'

'I don't give a fuck then what!'

'They'll lock you up in the mad house again! And this time it'll be for good!'

That got him. He stopped right there on the sidewalk, about twenty yards of which had by now entirely cleared.

'But you saw! You saw them!' he whined plaintively. To an onlooker he looked as though he was addressing some point on the ground a little way ahead of him. In reality he was looking at nothing. He was suddenly focusing all his attention on this inner voice, accepting its reality without question, fighting what it said but not the fact of its being there. I realised in that moment that I had accomplished what I needed to accomplish. We had a dialogue.

'Look,' I said, 'let's just get out of here before somebody calls the cops. You're behaving like a maniac. Look at that wrench you're waving around!'

He looked down at his hand as though it belonged to someone else, then he tossed the wrench on to the low wall that ran along the motel parking lot and sat down heavily next to it. I thought he was going to burst into tears, but he held them in. 'How could they?' he murmured. 'How could they?'

People were beginning to be curious now, their fear evaporating as they saw his rage subside. After all, he looked respectable enough, despite the dark glasses and the hat jammed oddly on his head. But they didn't get too close. The boldest gathered in a semi-circle at a safe distance, whispering among themselves about what they should do. The majority, as is usually the case, just gave him a wide berth and kept moving, anxious not to get involved.

My own main fear now was that the minor commotion he'd caused might have attracted the attention of Anne and Harold in their cabin just across the parking lot. I needn't have worried. Obviously they were too engrossed in whatever they were doing to pay attention to the world beyond their dusty cream venetian blinds. But I still had to get Richard away from there as fast as possible.

'Listen,' I said, 'this is your last chance to walk away from here. You stay, there are going to be cops, questions, probably you'll be arrested – which means your name on file! It's not smart. Now, haul ass!' That mention of his name on file triggered the response I needed. He passed his hands shakily over his face, got to his feet and, leaving the wrench where it lay, walked back across the street and disappeared into the parking lot of the 7-11. As we pulled out moments later in the rented car, a police patrol was arriving to check out the disturbance. The proprietor of a Chinese laundry had emerged from his shop and was pointing dramatically to the abandoned wrench on the wall and acting out a vigorous mime of Richard's eccentric comportment for the benefit of the officers. Nobody observed Richard, hat and glasses removed at my suggestion, driving off in the opposite direction.

'Ten more seconds,' I said, 'and you'd have been right in the middle of that. So just listen to me when I talk. That's all I ask. Just listen.'

'I think you'd better tell me,' he said with slow deliberation and a tremor of profound ontological fear in his voice, 'just what the fuck is going on.'

'First things first,' I said. 'There's no need to actually move your lips and use your voice when you want to talk to me. People will think you're talking to yourself, and we want to avoid attracting that kind of attention – right?'

'But what ... what do I do?' His voice cracked as he asked the question.

'You just think. I'm in your head, I can read your thoughts. I'll know when you want to talk to me. I'll also know when you don't, and I won't bother you unless I have to.'

'You mean you know everything I'm thinking?' He was

still talking aloud, staring straight ahead but driving on automatic pilot.

'Just about. Not everything exactly, because I can't be everywhere at once. The mind is a bigger place than its observer. And by "observer" I also mean the person to whom it belongs, not just an outsider like me. *You* don't know everything that's in your mind most of the time, do you? So how would you expect me to?' I thought it as well to emphasise this point so as to leave him at least some sense of privacy.

'This is so fucking weird.'

'Will you please try to say that without moving your lips? Just to please me?'

He tried. Very hard. The thought came over like a slowed-down tape recording with the volume turned way up. 'T-T-T-H-H-H-I-I-S-S-S I-I-S-S-S S-S-S-O-O-O-O F-F-F-U-U-C-K-I-I-N-N-G-G W-W-W-E-E-I-I-R-R-R-D-D !!!!'

'No need to try so hard. Just think like you normally think. I'll read you.'

He tried again. 'Is that better?'

'You're getting there.'

'Holy fucking Jesus, I don't believe this!'

'Listen,' I told him, 'you're not the only one who feels a little strange. Believe me, this isn't how I'd planned on spending my life either. To tell you the truth, I'm anxious to do something about it – and soon.'

'I need a drink,' he said.

'I don't think that's a good idea in your present frame of mind.'

'I don't give a fuck what you think!' he snapped back, pulling off the road and into the parking lot of a bar called 'The Bottom Line' that neither of us had been into before. 'Come on – I'll buy you one!' He thought the line but laughed out loud, a bitter, ugly laugh.

'Just be careful,' I said. 'You're angry, you're irrational, you're vulnerable. If you get drunk I can't help you. You're going to pick an argument or a fight just out of frustration, and you'll wind up getting the shit kicked out of you or worse.' I was really concerned about the way I could feel things going.

He pushed open the double door with a gunfighter's bravado and squinted to accustom his eyes to the gloom. The place was empty except for a sallow barman with greasy slicked-back hair and a body which seemed to fall in ever-looser folds from his forehead down.

'It's okay,' Richard said, 'there's nobody here anyway.'

'We tend to get a little busier between five and six,' said the barman, pushing aside the newspaper he'd been reading as though it were a heavy weight.

Richard realised that he'd spoken out loud again when he'd intended only to speak to me. It gave him a jolt. 'Give me a gin martini,' he said.

'Straight up, or on the rocks?'

'Straight up, with a twist.' He hauled himself on to a stool while the barman worked.

'It's okay,' he said to me, keeping the conversation properly internalised this time, 'I'm on top of it, I'm just going to have the one.' Then, as though to show both himself and me that he could handle the new-found complexity of his situation with perfect command, he said aloud to the barman: 'Have one yourself.'

'Thanks.' He dropped Richard's change into a jug on a shelf and pushed his martini across the bar top on a coaster. His professional sixth sense told him that this customer didn't want to talk, so he went back to his newspaper and left Richard to himself.

'If you can hold it down to one,' I said, trying not to nag, but feeling obliged none the less to press my case, 'that's fine. It'll help you relax and think straight. Two will screw you up. Believe me.'

Richard sipped his martini. It tasted good. He didn't answer me directly. His thoughts were moving too fast for me to follow them all. I wasn't even sure what direction he was taking through them. Eventually, however, he formed a clear sentence and aimed it in my direction. 'I thought you'd gone away, Rick. I thought I was cured.' There was a soulful, sad quality in the thought. I felt suddenly, unexpectedly, sorry for him.

'There was nothing to be cured of,' I told him as firmly as I could. 'You're as sane as the next man, and so am I.'

'I wouldn't like to have to persuade Roger Killanin of that.'

'You won't have to – not if you're sensible.'

'And what exactly does "sensible" mean in this context? Remembering not to mention to anybody that I'm nuts?'

'You're not nuts! Just get rid of that idea!'

'I'm talking to a voice in my head. That's nuts by anybody's definition!'

'Not necessarily. For one thing, I'm acting as a restraining influence on you right now. The voices that nuts hear tell them to kill people or blow up buildings. Have you ever heard of one saying he's got the Voice of Reason in his head, talking him out of doing something violent?'

He took the point grudgingly. 'I suppose you're right. I might have killed them both but for you.'

'And now you'd be sitting in jail watching the rest of your life go down the tubes.' I was pushing my advantage as hard as I could, trying to keep him under my control without provoking resentment.

'But you put me up to it,' he said suddenly, accusingly. 'You made me suspicious. It *was* you, wasn't it?'

'In a manner of speaking,' I admitted. I was anxious to play down this part of my role. 'I was the one who heard that phone call, not you. I guess I pointed you in a certain direction. Maybe I shouldn't have. If so, I'm sorry. But put yourself in my position. What would you have done?'

He thought this over. It was a reasonable point, and he was, despite all my reservations about him, a reasonable man. 'I guess I might have done the same. Anyway, that's history. The question is, what do we do now?'

'About them? In my view, nothing. Above all, nothing hasty. You know what I think? I think this affair is one of

86

those things that happens between friends who get too close and . . . something gets out of hand. I think Anne loves you. I think Harold in his way loves you. I'm willing to bet they both feel guilty as hell about this whole thing.'

'And that makes it all right?'

'Of course not. But sometimes a thing like this just has to run its course. Give it a chance to blow over. Human beings can do irrational, crazy, sometimes cruel things. They hurt people they don't want to hurt. Sometimes it's the people who get hurt who have to show some understanding – and, above all, some discretion.'

'I don't know how you expect me to forget this whole thing. Or forgive.'

'I don't. I'm just saying give it time. Give yourself time. I guarantee, whatever you do in haste you will live to regret.'

He finished his drink and sat there for a while, his mind still in turmoil. The barman, fortunately, was too indifferent even to ask him if he wanted another. He would certainly have said yes, a double, and that would have been bad news.

'Please believe me,' I said, 'I'm trying to persuade you what's best for you.' Actually it was true. I had come to realise that in his way, which wasn't quite my way, but near enough so I could sympathise with him, he did love her. Her faithfulness mattered deeply. He thought of her as an ally and a soul mate, just as he thought of Harold as someone whose friendship defined the meaning of the word.

And now this. It was, I knew, as close to unbearable for him as it would have been in my world for me. 'Whatever has happened,' I went on, 'you can only make it worse by going berserk and tearing your life up by the roots.'

I didn't know what else to say. I could do no more for him. I tried to read his thoughts, but they were swamped in such a torrent of pain and confusion that it was impossible. So I let him be.

After a while he made an effort – in fact, I'm forced to say, an heroic effort – to pull himself together. He pushed away his empty glass and slid off his stool. 'I'll give it a try,' he said aloud, unthinking, and started for the exit.

'You do that, pal,' said the barman, not even glancing up from his paper.

That night they were going to a fund-raiser for the opera. When Anne got home Richard was in the shower. When she entered the bathroom, he was in the dressing room getting into his tuxedo. By the time she started dressing he was watching the evening news in the bedroom, but by the time she sat down before her mirror he had moved into the living room. Somewhere along the way they kissed briefly and lied about their day.

In the car he put Vivaldi on the CD. Outwardly he was calm and a little bored, as she might have expected, by the prospect of the evening ahead. Inwardly both he and I were marvelling at Anne's cool self-control. There she was, fresh (if that was the word) from the ithyphallic delights of Balthazar's Motel, her senses presumably still resonating from those hours of fierce, adulterous carnality, now sitting next to him in the car and chatting inconsequentially about Mabel Dodge-Bryan's seating plan and how it had had to be revised five times as several big cheques for the building fund came in late.

'It's just possible, isn't it,' I found myself thinking, 'that nothing untoward was actually going on between them? Aren't we jumping to conclusions on relatively little evidence?'

This had been a private reflection and not meant for Richard, but when a loud snort of incredulity burst involuntarily from his lips I realised that he was becoming almost as deft at reading my thoughts as I was his.

Anne looked at him, startled, and he tried to disguise the outburst as a coughing fit. 'Are you all right?' she asked, with genuine-seeming concern. He assured her he was, and blew his nose unnecessarily, while growling inwardly at me: 'You're crazier than I am if you think that!'

I hurriedly apologised for the thought, and congratulated him on his alertness. 'Incidentally,' I continued, 'there's one thing we should talk about before we arrive. Harold's going to be there tonight.' I only knew this because he knew it, and I was aware that he had pushed the fact to the back of his mind. I thought it better we should deal with it and be prepared for the encounter.

'I haven't forgotten,' he informed me brusquely.

'Hadn't you better decide how you're going to behave towards him?'

'I'll behave just as I always do.'

'Okay. I'm sure you'll handle it.' I would have liked to have felt more sure, but thought it better to boost his confidence rather than undermine it by harping on the point. In the event, I must say that he was as good as his word. He and Harold, fortunately, only had time to exchange the briefest of greetings before he was whisked off by Mabel Dodge-Bryan to meet the guest of honour, a short, pinch-faced Hungarian conductor whose features he had seen on the covers of record albums, compact discs and scandal sheets for as long as he could remember.

At dinner Richard was seated on the top table between a UN Ambassador's widow, reputedly worth three billion, and the conductor's charming twenty-one-year-old sixth wife. Anne was prestigiously seated a few places along on the conductor's left. Harold was on a more modest secondary table. Throughout the evening Richard kept a discreet watch on both of them, looking for knowing glances, little smiles, or any of the tell-tale signs of secret intimacy. But there was nothing.

'You've got to hand it to them,' he said to me, 'they're very good.'

I agreed. It was impressive. Credit where credit's due.

The drive home was uneventful. Anne announced that she was tired – he resisted an impulse to say he wasn't surprised – and put her seat back and closed her eyes. Forty minutes later they were in bed, Anne already asleep, and

Richard staring up at what little he could see of the ceiling. I remained absolutely quiet, in a state of something like suspended animation. I didn't want to start up a conversation and hoped he wouldn't. But after a while his thoughts began to cast around in search of me.

'Rick? Are you there?'

'Of course I'm here.'

'Can I talk to you?'

'Why don't you try to get some sleep?'

'I can't.'

I knew what was coming and I really didn't want to get into it. But I had no choice. I let him tell me in his own way.

'I've got such a hard-on. A real fucking boner.'

I was aware of that, and told him so.

'Well?'

'Well what? I don't know what you expect me to do about it.'

'What do you think I should do?'

'I don't know. You could jerk off very quietly without waking her.'

'I'm embarrassed with you there.'

'You don't have to be – but I understand. Try thinking about something else.'

'I can't. I want . . . I want . . . '

'I know what you want.'

'I can't help it. I'm disgusted by myself, but I want her. I can't help it.'

I'd been afraid this would happen and still, frankly, wasn't sure how to handle the situation. I decided to meet it head on.

'You could wake her up. You know she usually likes that.'

'I can't! Not after what's happened.'

'It's up to you. I'm staying out of this.'

A lengthy silence. Then: 'I'd think she was just humouring me.'

'So – maybe you should let her humour you.'

'You think?'

'Where's the harm?' I was far from being as relaxed about it as I wanted him to think. It was a risk but, to be honest, part of me was curious. In fact, to be brutally honest, pruriently so.

He turned towards her, slipped his hands under her flimsy night-dress and began softly massaging her body. She stirred, gave a little moan, and moved towards him. 'Mmmmmm, that's nice . . . ' she whispered drowsily. I could tell from the sound that her mouth was turned up in that little cat-like smile she had when she was feeling sexy.

'What is it honey, can't you . . . oh.' She had felt his erection. She snuggled closer to him, running her hands back and forth along its length and making little breathy whispering noises. He was glad it was dark. He wouldn't have wanted to see her eyes. I could hear him breathing faster as she slipped down under the covers and took him in her mouth.

I hunched into the shadows of his consciousness and, if I'd had any teeth, would have been clenching them. I began to wish I hadn't allowed this to happen.

When it was over she snaked up his body and nestled her face contentedly into the gap between his shoulder and his neck, sighed happily, and went back to sleep.

He lay still. He was tense, not knowing what to say to me. I thought I'd better break the silence.

'Well,' I said, rather feebly, 'that was all right.' I hoped he didn't sense the equivocalness in my tone.

'She serviced me.' The reply was flat, bitter, full of resentment. I tried to make the best of things.

'I thought it was very generous of her.'

'D'you think she was thinking about him?'

'I don't know. It doesn't matter. Don't think about it.'

'How can I not?'

'You can try. I'll help you.'

'How can you?' he demanded with sudden bitterness.

'You don't exist. You're just a symptom of shock, like the last time. Either you'll go away or I'll go mad again. I know that.'

I realised I had to do something. If I let him lie there all night brooding like this, heaven knows what frame of mind he could be in by dawn. 'Suppose I can prove I'm real?' I said impulsively.

He was a little taken aback by the boldness of this. 'How?' he asked eventually, half fearing that the madness had already engulfed him.

'If I can show you something that I know and you don't, would that convince you?'

'That depends,' he said cautiously, his mind a no-man's-land of uncertainty and deep suspicion.

I jumped in quickly. 'All right,' I said, 'forget the problems of proving something without external references. Like I keep saying, just take things one step at a time. I probably can't do it all in one night, but we can make a start. You're going to need a flashlight, two pieces of cardboard, scissors and some Scotch tape.'

Twenty minutes later we were all set up in his den. The flashlight was wedged horizontally between two paperweights on the edge of his desk. It was pointing at a piece of stiff cardboard that was being held up by filing cabinet drawers to serve as a screen.

About three feet behind this cardboard screen was a second one held up in the same way. The only difference between them was that in the first screen Richard had cut, under my instructions, two narrow vertical slits which could be opened or closed by two flaps of cardboard on hinges of Scotch tape.

He stepped back to regard it quizzically.

'It may not look like much,' I said, 'but you have just built a serious piece of experimental laboratory equipment. Now, switch off the overhead light and switch on the flashlight.'

The flashlight's beam cut through the darkness and hit

the first screen, showing both slits closed. 'Open one of the slits,' I said. 'It doesn't matter which.'

He opened one. On the second screen now we saw a narrow, sharp-edged strip of light corresponding to the shape of the open slit in the first screen.

'So far so good,' I said. 'That's exactly what we would have expected to see, isn't it?' I waited for his assent before continuing. 'Now,' I said, 'suppose we ask ourselves the question, what would we expect to see on the second screen if we were to open *both* slits in the first screen at the same time? Logically you would expect to see two strips of light like the one you see now – right?'

'I guess,' he grunted, wondering what possible relevance all this could have to his problems.

'Well, let's see what actually happens. Open the second slit, would you?' He leaned over and did so. 'Now, would you care to describe what you see?'

What in fact he saw, in place of the two separate strips of light that he might logically have anticipated, was a wide pattern of dark and light strips shading into one another. It was a remarkably clear demonstration of the point I had been hoping to make, and I was frankly more than a little disappointed by his response.

'I'll tell you so fucking what!' I replied a touch sharply. 'It's irrational. It doesn't make any sense. When one slit is open you get a thin strip of light on the second screen, but when both are open you get this complex pattern. Why? Have you any idea?'

'Who knows? Reflection or something.'

'No, it isn't reflection. It's much more fundamental than that.'

'So tell me.'

'May we just establish for the record', I said, determined to drive my main point home, 'that, had you thought about it, you would not have anticipated this result with both slits open at the same time?'

'Okay, okay! So what's the big deal? Jesus!'

'Therefore,' I plowed on, 'I have shown you something that you did not already know, but which I did know.'

'I can only give a limited yes on that,' he said grudgingly. 'How do I know I didn't already know it unconsciously?'

'Okay, fair point. But I'm now going to tell you something else you don't know, which is *why* this happens. The reason is that when only one slit was open the light was behaving like it was made up of particles, kind of like tiny bullets or golf balls being fired through the opening in straight lines. But when we opened both slits at the same time, the light changed its mind and started behaving like waves. Try it again, close one slit,' he did so, 'and it goes back to behaving like particles.' Once again a single sharp-edged strip of light appeared on the second screen. 'Open the second slit . . . and we have waves.'

'Riveting.'

'Save your sarcasm and try asking an intelligent question.'

'Is this a cure for insomnia?'

'Okay, I'll ask it for you. The question is how does the light going through the first slit know whether the second one is open or not? It obviously does, because when the second slit is closed the light going through the first behaves like particles. But when the second one is open, the light going through both behaves like waves. So who tells the light going through the first slit whether the second one is open or not?'

Silence. Then: 'There's a catch here somewhere.'

'You have just demonstrated the fundamental paradox at the heart of quantum theory.'

'I have?'

'Actually *I* have. Check it out, you'll find I'm right.'

'It's still not conclusive proof that you're who you say you are.'

'We'll get there. For now you can take some comfort from the fact that you're no crazier than the rest of the universe – so get some sleep.'

6

'WITH THIS BABY you'll pick up every word in a room fifty feet square.' The man had a face that was wide, soft and utterly without character, but which, as though by way of compensation, was set in a permanent scowl of surly hostility toward the world in general. His eyes looked out defensively from folds of flesh, alert to insult or offence. To his customers he projected the feeling that they were privileged to get this close without being hit – and they still better not fuck with him.

Richard had no intention of doing anything of the sort. He took the tiny microphone from the man's thick fingers and examined it. It was hardly larger than a pin.

'You position your transmitter within fifty yards, then you can listen in up to five, ten miles away.'

'I don't want to listen in directly,' Richard said. 'I just want to record whatever people are saying in the vicinity.'

'Voice activated – no problem. You set your transmitter like this,' he flipped a switch, 'and either connect your recording device direct via this socket, or transmit and record from your receiver.'

Richard opted for the simpler method of recording direct. He figured he would either use a car parked near the motel, or maybe even rent another cabin on a permanent basis and install the recorder there. Getting the microphone into cabin nine he was sure would present no problems.

The fat man liked people who paid cash, as Richard did.

'Anything else you need, directional mikes, hidden cameras, they do amazing stuff with fibre optics now . . . '

'I think this'll be fine,' Richard said, taking the plastic carrier in which his purchases were wrapped. 'I'll be back if I need anything more.'

'Hey, mister – ?' Richard paused halfway to the door. The fat man was looking at him with a kind of clumsy meaningfulness, trying to communicate a man-to-man understanding that any problems Richard might have could all be taken care of with the help of this establishment. 'Need a firearm? We have outstanding weaponry.'

Richard glanced over towards the half of the shop where rifles, shotguns and handguns of all description were on display. I felt him tempted, but then he pulled back. 'I already have one,' he said, and went out the door. It was a lie, but I was glad he told it. I only regretted that I'd failed to talk him out of this idea of bugging Anne and Harold at the motel. No one, I had told him, hears good of themselves by eavesdropping.

'I'm not interested in hearing about myself,' he had replied. 'I want to hear about them. I want to know if you're right and this thing isn't serious.'

'And if it is?' I inquired, not wanting to go back on what I'd said, but at least allowing for the possibility of being wrong.

'If it is . . . well, then, I'll take it from there. And I mean *I'll* take it – without any help from you. So keep your damn nose out!'

That was all I could get out of him. He was learning with an alarming swiftness how to screen his thoughts from me. I could still read his mind, I knew the choices he faced, but I could not predict with any certainty the direction he would take. In a way this was healthy. It meant that he was increasingly accepting me as a reality, someone to be reckoned with, related to, and when necessary outwitted. But it did not make my task of maintaining control any easier.

He had been obliged to spend the morning with a group of associates with whom he was building a new condominium on the site of a remarkably fine art deco theatre. It was a moment for some self-congratulation on the way in which the planning watchdogs and preservationists had been successfully outflanked. Richard, however, was not in a celebratory mood. He explained away his glumness by claiming toothache, which also got him out of the otherwise obligatory lunch. I had wanted him to use the spare time by going to a library or book shop where he would find a simple introduction to quantum physics so that we could continue our discussion of the previous night, but we had wound up in this disagreeable establishment buying an electronic bugging device. It was obviously pointless trying to argue with him, so I settled quietly into the remotest spot I could find at the back of his mind and pointedly ignored him for a while.

'Quit sulking.' The injunction took me by surprise. We were in his car, I realised, waiting at a stop light. He was watching the reflection of his own eyes in his rear-view mirror. There was a little crinkle of amusement at their corners.

'I am not sulking,' I replied firmly, wanting him to know that I resented the imputation.

'Come on – you sound like you've got a stick up your ass.'

I didn't reply. But I realised, of course, that this was his awkward way of apologising for his earlier behaviour. I decided to let bygones be bygones. The lights changed and he drove on.

'Anyway,' I said eventually, 'if I were sulking, which I'm not, I'd have every right to be.'

'How come?'

'You accused me of wanting to interfere in your life – when all I want is to get out of it! But I can't do that without a little more cooperation from you than I'm getting right now.'

'What d'you want me to do?'

I knew exactly what I wanted him to do. I also knew how reluctant he would be to comply. 'I want you to make an appointment with Emma Todd.'

He took a moment to absorb this before answering. 'I thought you were trying to persuade me that I'm sane. Now you're asking me to see a shrink. Isn't it about time you made up your mind?'

'I'm not asking *you* to see her,' I said. '*I'm* the one who needs to talk to her. Unfortunately I can't do that without your help.'

'Wait a minute,' he said, 'let me get this straight. You're asking me to go to a shrink and say, "It isn't for myself, but there's this voice in my head wants to talk to you"? You're nuts! I'd never get out of there – except in a strait-jacket!'

'It won't be like the last time,' I assured him. 'The problem then was that neither of us knew what was happening. We were both in a state of disorientation where it took only the slightest provocation to set us at each other's throats. That can't happen again. All we have to do is stay calm and behave properly. We can say anything we like so long as we behave like sane, normal human beings. Well, *a* sane, normal human being.'

He was not convinced. I soldiered on in an attempt to bridge the gap between us.

'The reason I have to do this,' I explained, 'is that an idea came to me during those hypnosis sessions that we had with her. I think there is a way back into my other life, and I think she can help me find it.'

'So why didn't you bring it up then?'

'Because the only thing that mattered then was getting you back on your feet and out of there. I had to pretend I was an illness of which you were being cured. And I'm here to tell you that's a pretty humiliating position to be in!'

I felt him smirk. The notion of my predicament for some reason amused him. I bit back my response, but he felt it none the less. 'All right,' he said, 'don't get shirty. You have to admit it's pretty funny.'

'So are a lot of things in retrospect,' I said. 'However, since I put myself through all that to protect you, maybe now you'll be good enough to return the favour.'

He didn't answer directly. 'You think there's something special about this woman, don't you?' he said, reading my thoughts. 'I think you're wrong,' he continued without waiting for me to comment, 'I don't trust her.'

I didn't want to discuss Emma with him. There was little point in trying to explain the level on which she and I had communicated while he had been in deep trance. 'If I'm wrong, I'm wrong,' I said. 'If I'm right, I'll be gone — and you'll have your life to yourself again. It's got to be worth a try.'

'I'm not sure I trust you any more than I trust her.'

'You're still not convinced I'm real, are you?' I sighed wearily. 'I thought I'd persuaded you last night.' We had, in the sleepless hours before dawn, gone on to discuss some of the further mysteries of quantum physics, using the example of our two-slit experiment to illustrate the dual wave/particle nature of the fundamental building blocks of all reality. He had been moving towards an acceptance of the multiple universe theory when exhaustion finally overcame him and he fell asleep. Now, apparently, it had all been for nothing.

'You can check out what I said in any book on quantum physics, which is what I've been asking you to do. It's hardly my fault if you're too lazy to read!'

He bridled indignantly at this and I realised I had gone too far. He knew that I considered myself more intelligent than him and resented it. It was my turn to apologise. 'I'm not implying you're stupid,' I told him, 'so get off that high horse. I have an advantage on you merely because one of the magazines I happen to publish in my universe is called *Particle/Wave*, which deals with this kind of stuff, and more. As a matter of fact . . . '

An idea hit me like a brick on the head. Why hadn't I thought of it before? Tickelbakker!

'Listen, the guy who came to me with the idea for the

magazine was doing research at the university right here in the city. It's very likely that he's still here ... ' I checked myself. I was starting to use language loosely. 'I don't mean "still", I mean also. I should think, because of the degree of similarity between our two universes, that he's also here. It would be easy for you to check. His name's Tickelbakker. Dr Michael J. Tickelbakker. There aren't too many Tickelbakkers around, so it shouldn't be difficult. Just ask for him at the University Physics department.'

Richard took the information in. He was, I could tell, prepared to consider the suggestion, but just now, as we pulled on to the forecourt of Balthazar's Motel, his mind was moving on to other things.

The manager of Balthazar's was called Cy, and Richard's assumptions about the place turned out to have been remarkably accurate. Fifty dollars went a long way towards loosening up Cy's tongue, and another fifty ensured that he knew where his loyalties lay.

Cabin nine, we ascertained, had been the regular love-nest of 'Mr Smith' and his companion for slightly more than three months – in fact, since just after Richard came out of the clinic. The timing seemed to support my thesis that this was an affair started under the pressure of Richard's illness and liable to run its course if left undisturbed.

'You don't *know* that,' he persisted, 'any more than I do. But I *want* to know – and I intend to.'

There was no further argument. Cy handed over the key to cabin nine, which was, he said, kept on permanent reservation by 'Mr Smith' for whenever he and his companion chose to make use of it – which was, to the best of Cy's knowledge, three or four times a week.

Richard silently computed the aggregate number of times per week that Anne was currently having sex. He allowed for the fact that she was probably enjoying two, maybe three bouts per session with Harold – which was most likely the case while the affair remained at its height – and was inwardly shocked by the total when added to the amount she was still enjoying with him. I made no comment.

The room itself was a classic of vulgarity. Upmarket though the establishment was, there is in some markets only so far up you can go. The ceiling mirror was tinted pink and the queen-size bed draped in some white fluffy material that looked like washable nylon. But the sheets were clean and the whole place in good order. At the foot of the bed stood a 27-inch television which Richard flipped on with the auto-control he picked up from the built-in headboard and bedside cabinets. It was pre-tuned to the closed-circuit porn channel. He switched it off without even a flicker of interest in the writhing images.

'This is no one-off affair,' he murmured silently, 'it's pure sex! If she can do this with him, she can do it with anybody.'

'Don't brood on it,' I said. 'Just do what you have to do and let's get out of here.'

First, however, he insisted on checking out the adjoining bathroom. It had a double jacuzzi set into a recess with a shower attachment overhead. Over the hand basin was a single mirrored cabinet. I was wishing he wouldn't open it, but he did. It contained half a dozen varieties of love oil, all half used. He removed the cap of one and was almost sick from the overpoweringly sweet smell of chemically scented strawberries. It was too much. He sat down on the edge of the lime-green jacuzzi and wept.

I remained silent. What could I say? But my heart went out to him.

'I'm sorry,' he said after a few moments, 'I didn't mean to do that. I'm okay.'

'I know you are,' I said. 'Come on, let's go.'

He planted the tiny microphone in the side of the headboard where it would be unlikely to be disturbed by maids. Then he made a generous deal with Cy, renting cabin fifteen by the week and with a hundred a week on the side for Cy to guarantee his discretion. He attached the cassette recorder to the transmitter and left them in an identical bedside cabinet to the one in cabin nine.

In the car neither of us spoke for a while. Then he said, 'My whole life's a sham. Not just my marriage, my life.'

'Richard,' I began, choosing my words carefully, 'right now you've no better friend than me. I know how you feel, truly. But before you judge her, just remember that night that you told her about me. Well, I suppose *I* told her, or a mixture of us both. It was before we sorted ourselves out properly. But remember when you heard her on the phone next morning, sobbing her heart out at the prospect of having to commit you to that clinic. You can't pretend that wasn't real. You can't pretend she didn't love you then.'

'How d'you know she wasn't doing it just to impress them at the other end?' he said flatly. 'Secretly she was probably overjoyed. She probably thought she'd got rid of me for good.'

'You don't know that,' I said, 'and as long as you don't know it you mustn't say it.' But I wished I felt as sure of myself as I was trying to sound.

'Thanks for the effort, Rick,' he said, 'but I know how you really feel. I know you're wondering if you knew *your* Anne any better than I knew mine. I want to say something about that. I think your Anne was all right. I feel it. I get that feeling from you. I can tell that your relationship was better than ours. You shared more. There was no pretence. Yours was the world where that relationship worked. Maybe the only one. Maybe there's only one where every relationship really works – or at least where it worked as well as yours did.'

I was so moved by this unselfish effort to reassure me in the depths of his own despair that I couldn't say anything for a while.

'Don't worry,' he said, 'you don't have to – say anything, I mean.'

How wrong I'd been about this man. The injustice of my first opinion of him was almost unbearable.

'No, you weren't wrong,' he went on softly. 'Everything you thought about me was perfectly justified. You got your life right, I got mine wrong. I had cheap dreams. That's all I shared with her – cheap dreams. Making money, being somebody. Well, you get back what you put in. I guess that's a rule everywhere, including where you come from.' He gave a little dry laugh.

'I'll tell you something else,' he went on, needing to talk now, so I let him. 'About Harold. Your Harold was a real friend. I know that because that's what you looked for in him. Me? I thought, hey, that's neat, this kid I grew up with has turned into a smart lawyer, that's going to be useful to me. You see the difference? He was your friend first and somebody who was useful second. With me it was the other way around. It's like a reverse image in a mirror – one of those old ghost stories. I'm the nightmare version of your life.'

'You're too hard on yourself,' I said. 'I know you don't think so now, but you'll get over this. One thing I am sure of – I don't know why, but I am – is that nothing's written in stone. You can change things. You can change yourself.'

'You sound like one of those moronic Californian self-help cults,' he said, not accusingly. I didn't take offence.

'At least one good thing's happened,' I said. 'You seem to have started to really believe in me.'

'I'm trying to,' he said, 'and I want to. What was the name you mentioned before, that guy at the university? Stickerbottle?'

'Tickelbakker. Dr Michael J. Tickelbakker.'

'But what do I say to him? What questions do I ask?'

'Don't worry – I'll feed you the right questions.'

'And what do I tell him about why I want to talk to him in the first place?'

'I don't know.' I hadn't thought about this, and should

have. 'Tell him you're doing research for a book you're writing,' I suggested lamely.

'Are you kidding? I'm in real estate.'

'So? People in real estate can write a book if they want to.'

'You think? Most of them are so illiterate they think "Moby Dick" is a sexually transmitted disease.'

I smiled to myself. 'Tell that to Tickelbakker, if you find him. He'll enjoy it.'

In the event it proved unnecessary to offer any reason for meeting up with Tickelbakker aside from inviting him to lunch at Chez Arnaud, the best restaurant for miles around in Richard's universe as well as my own. The fact that Anne was on a committee to finance some new endowment at the university was sufficient of an introduction, and I remembered only too well how much Tickelbakker enjoyed good food and fine wine.

He was, for me, a joy to behold, even at second hand through Richard's eyes. He entered the restaurant wearing, as far as I could make out, the same crumpled tweed jacket he had worn on the last occasion I had seen him. He moved and waved his arms in the same gangling, unco-ordinated way, and, despite being six feet tall and in his mid-thirties, he looked as always about twelve. His hair was baby-blond and thinning, except for an egregiously preserved lock that curled over his forehead. Clear-rimmed glasses rested on an upturned nose that you somehow imagined was freckled even though it wasn't. His eyes were round and bright with eagerness and, even though he was not in fact smiling broadly all the time, you somehow got the impression, as with his non-existent freckles, that he was.

Cheerfully ignoring Richard's abstemious order of salad, grilled sole and mineral water, Tickelbakker, sipping a glass of champagne and taking Richard at his word when invited to order whatever he wanted, embarked upon a lunch of such indulgence that Richard silently marvelled at the robustness of his constitution, while blanching inwardly at the mounting cost coming his way. 'It's all right,' I reassured him, 'he's worth every cent – believe me.'

It was the day after our visit to the motel. The previous evening had passed off without incident between Anne and Richard. He had dined with two bankers from Chicago who were key investors in one of his developments, while Anne had said she was seeing someone for a preliminary chat about a Christmas gala they were organising for cancer research. A discreet call to Cy from the restaurant where Richard was dining had confirmed that the motel had not featured on her itinerary that evening.

There had been no sex between them overnight, and practically no conversation. In the morning she had left the apartment by seven to go to her aerobics workout while he was still in his shower. He had spent the morning on desultory paper work in his office, having given instructions that he was not to be disturbed. What he was actually doing was rehearsing with me a sufficient layman's knowledge (which was all I had to offer) of quantum physics in order to be able to present himself to Tickelbakker as a well-off dilettante in search of intellectual stimulation.

'That's very impressive,' Tickelbakker said, beaming over his escalope de foie gras à la vinaigrette and accompanying glass of Sauterne. Richard had just come to the end of his carefully prepared pitch. 'That's as good a lay description as I've come across of the basic principles.'

Richard enjoyed a little glow of pride and we exchanged secret congratulations: he on the clarity of my exposition, I on the excellence of his memory. He had started off with my favourite illustration of the scale on which we were talking. Imagine the earth stuffed with grapes, and that's how many atoms there are in a baseball. Now imagine a speck of dust in the centre of a baseball pitch, and that's the nucleus of the atom. Finally imagine another speck of dust on the boundary line, and that's an electron circling the nucleus.

'As I understand it,' he went on, 'it's on this level that

the fun really starts. These sub-atomic entities, electrons, neutrons, whatever, behave both as particles and waves just as one sees in the two-slit experiment with light.'

'Exactly. You can do the same experiment – it's a classic – using streams of electrons or neutrons instead of your flashlight beam and you'll get the same result.'

'What I don't fully understand,' said Richard, 'is why. What's the explanation of this particle/wave duality?'

'You're not alone in that. Because effectively there is no definitive explanation.'

'Another thing I find equally fascinating and baffling,' Richard, prompted by me, prompted him, 'is the way these electrons or protons or whatever seem to know when we're observing them and adjust their behaviour accordingly.'

'Mm-hm,' Tickelbakker nodded, eyeing the bottle of La Lagune '72 that was being opened in anticipation of his aile de volaille aux poireaux et truffes. 'For instance, take a stream of electrons going through both open slits in your two-slit experiment and therefore giving you a wave pattern on the second screen. Let's suppose you want to measure the exact position of one of those electrons while it's behaving like a wave, or say you want to find out which of the two slits it goes through. We have techniques for doing that with absolute accuracy. There is no problem recording what's going on at that level. The problem is that the electron seems to know it's being observed and suddenly stops what it's doing. It lets you take a picture of it going through one slit or the other, but in that instant it stops being a wave and becomes a particle and slams into that second screen like it's a bullet – just as it would if only one slit were open.'

'Okay – so how does it know it's being watched?'

'That's where we get into some really fancy theories.'

'Such as,' I lobbed the words with careful precision into Richard's mind, 'the Many Worlds theory developed by Hugh Everett at Princeton in 1957. Go ahead, say it!'

'Such as,' Richard ventured tentatively, 'the Many Worlds theory developed by Hugh Everett at Princeton in 1957.'

'Yes, indeed!' said Tickelbakker. 'My word, Mr Hamilton, you really do know something about this subject, don't you!'

'Not really,' Richard replied modestly. 'I'm not a mathematician, so I have to take it on trust that the equations work. But I understand that the implications of this theory are staggering.' Each word had been dictated by me a split second before he spoke it. We were becoming quite a double act. More importantly, he was now convinced beyond any shadow of doubt that the information pouring out of him had its origins elsewhere than in his own unconscious. My credentials were finally becoming unimpeachably established with him.

'What Everett said, as I understand it,' he continued, lifting the words directly from me like a newscaster reading from his autocue, 'is that instead of a wave becoming a particle when we look at it, what actually happens is that the person doing the looking splits into two identical selves, the only difference between them being that one of them is looking at a wave, and the other is looking at a particle.'

'Exactly! Plus they're doing it in two totally separate universes!'

'So every time a scientist in a laboratory looks at an electron or whatever, the universe splits into two?' I had deliberately fed him a misleading question here in order to impress on him even further the enormity of what I wanted him to understand.

'No, no,' Tickelbakker corrected him, as I knew he would, 'it's quite independent of scientists or anybody else. It's called quantum transition, and it's going on incessantly in every star, every galaxy, every corner of the universe. Remember – *everything* is made out of this same stuff!'

'So every time one of these "transitions" occurs, the whole universe splits into two versions of itself – in one of which there is a wave inside one part of one atom, and in the other there's a particle instead. And that will be the only difference between those two universes?'

'That's about the size of it.'

'But it's utterly insane!' The protest came spontaneously from Richard with no prompting from me. It was a healthy reaction and I was curious to see how Tickelbakker countered it.

He laughed. 'Niels Bohr, who pioneered this work back in the twenties, said that if you weren't shocked by quantum theory, then you had failed to understand it.'

'But that means there must be an infinite number of universes.'

'Not quite infinite. It's limited mathematically. But for practical purposes – yes, infinite.'

'So in other words,' Richard went on, reading once more from his internal autocue, 'while you and I are sitting here in this restaurant, a virtually identical you and I are also sitting in a virtually identical restaurant in a virtually identical universe – and so on ad infinitum.'

'In some of those universes you and I, I'm sorry to say, are not having lunch.' Tickelbakker poked appreciatively at a ripe-looking brie and said he would have some of that along with a piece of fine English stilton, and maybe a glass of the Warre '45 to go with them. 'In some of them,' he continued with a note of genuine regret, 'we haven't even met. In some of them we haven't even been born. In some of them, however, we probably know each other much better.'

'For instance,' I interrupted, seizing on the opportunity to drive home my point with Richard, 'in one of them I might be a magazine publisher instead of a real estate developer, and you might be editing a magazine for me called *Particle/Wave*.'

Tickelbakker laughed. 'Why not? Sounds like a fine idea. As a matter of fact I've often thought of trying to put some kind of magazine together for the slightly better than layman reader. I think there's a gap in the market. But I haven't found a publisher.'

'But where exactly are all these parallel universes?' I asked, moving on quickly before getting side-tracked into a venture that I knew was close to Tickelbakker's heart.

'That, I have to admit, is a little hard to describe without actually using mathematics. When we use a description like parallel universe we tend to think in everyday commonsense terms of something like a railroad track branching off into two, then three, then four tracks, and so on, but all going forward through the same four-dimensional (three of space, one of time) framework.' He looked up at the hovering waiter and, to Richard's astonishment, declined dessert.

'In actual fact,' he continued, 'when we talk of parallel universes we don't literally mean parallel at all. First of all we have to think in terms of many more dimensions than the four we are familiar with. This, I'm afraid, is where the language of mathematics comes in. Because that's what it is – a language of considerably more sophistication and precision than mere words. The nearest I can get to describing it in words would be to say that these other universes split off at right angles to our own – a virtually infinite number of right angles, which in turn could only exist in superspace and supertime, which are mathematical concepts.'

There seemed little more to be said. Richard and I were both silent for a moment as Tickelbakker savoured the 12-year-old Macallan malt that he had chosen in preference to a Cognac with his coffee.

Then Richard, taking me by surprise and seizing the initiative, leaned forward and fixed Tickelbakker with his best down-to-earth, man-to-man gaze.

'Now look,' he began, 'just between the two of us, do you believe all this stuff? Or is it just so much hot air?'

Tickelbakker gave an amiably patient grin, fully comprehending (well, not *quite* fully) the enormity of what Richard was attempting to grasp.

'Belief doesn't really come into it,' he replied thoughtfully. 'When you confront a theory of any kind, whether it's relativity, quantum physics, or just the proposition that the sun will rise tomorrow morning, you ask yourself whether it's compatible with the known facts. If it is, you work with it.'

'Even if it sounds palpably ludicrous?'

'What was that line in one of the Sherlock Holmes stories? "Once you have eliminated the impossible, then whatever remains, however improbable, must be the truth." The truth in an absolute sense is maybe putting it a little high, because we don't deal in absolute truths. We leave that to the theologians and witch doctors. But I can tell you, a lot of very smart people accept the Many Worlds theory as the most likely explanation of why quantum mechanics — which we rely on daily in everything from micro-chips to lasers and the television tube — is the way it is. Even some of the people who build those things don't fully realise that they're building them with materials possessing no more ultimate tangibility than a thought passing through their brain.

'It is, as has often been remarked in other contexts,' he concluded in a serene glow of post-prandial contentment, 'a funny old world.'

7

WHEN EMMA TODD came on the line Richard told her that he had to see her as soon as possible. No, it wasn't exactly an emergency, but he did need to discuss something with her. She said she could make room around six at her private office and gave him the address. He said he'd be there.

He spent the rest of the afternoon at his desk dealing with paperwork. He even took a call from Harold and discussed with complete equanimity a bank loan they were negotiating with two partners for the purchase of a prime site in the financial district. His tone of voice gave away nothing of his emotional state, which bothered me. I was uneasy about this ability to shut his feelings off like a tap, but I said nothing.

Emma's private office was in an ugly building constructed in the fifties but with a fine central location. Richard remembered he had tried to buy it a couple of years ago, but the owners had finally changed their minds and decided to hang on to it for a few years more, by which time its value might well have tripled. He had been furious, but now it seemed a forgotten and unimportant disappointment.

The doorman called Emma's receptionist. Richard took the elevator. On the third floor he followed the arrows towards the rear of the building where the less expensive apartments were to be found because there was no view. At one minute to six he presented himself to Emma's pleasant, sixty-ish receptionist, who asked him to wait for a moment while she disappeared through a ripple-glass door.

Richard sat down and surveyed the drab, functional little waiting room with its low central table, well-thumbed magazines and locked filing cabinets. The only splash of colour was provided by a vase of red and white tulips on the end of the receptionist's desk. I wondered whether she or Emma was responsible for them. I also wondered if this office was part of Emma's private apartment. Richard chimed in that it almost certainly was. He knew the size of these apartments. They were surprisingly large for the time at which they had been built. I wondered if Emma lived alone.

The receptionist returned and asked Richard to step through to Emma's office. It was a comfortable size and had an informal atmosphere, but there was something odd about it that Richard couldn't put his finger on. Then I realised what it was: there were no books, just stacks of heavy folders, some open and showing braille pages.

Emma was standing by her desk, listening for her visitor's entry. When she heard the door she held out her hand and gave her composed yet guilelessly welcoming, warm smile. As they exchanged greetings Richard observed a golden labrador with a blind person's harness sleeping in a corner. 'I hope you don't mind dogs,' she said. 'If you do, he's quite happy to go sleep in the apartment. He can sleep anywhere.' Richard said on the contrary he was very fond of dogs, though he didn't have one himself. Emma invited him to take a seat.

'It's very good of you to make time to see me,' Richard began as Emma settled behind her desk. 'I'm not having any problems, but I think you may be able to help me. I find myself still dogged sometimes by this feeling that — '

He broke off as he saw Emma's hand reach out to switch on the cassette recorder on her desk. She had made no effort to conceal the gesture and realised at once why he had stopped.

'You prefer I didn't use this?' she asked.

'I think I would, if that's all right.'

'It's just that it helps me with my case notes. But if I understand what you're saying, we don't have a "case" here.'

'I don't believe so,' he said with a light laugh, 'but I shall defer to your judgment.' I was impressed by the way he was handling this, and told him so. He thanked me and said he was going to let me take over as soon as he'd finished his introductory remarks.

'It may be my imagination,' he went on, 'or some residual post traumatic echo – you'll have to forgive me, I don't know any of the proper terms for all of this.'

'You're doing fine,' Emma reassured him. 'Just tell me in your own words.'

'Well, it's just that I get this feeling, nothing more than that, that I haven't shaken quite as free of this other life, this imaginary "Rick" persona, as I'd like to. It's not that I'm hearing voices or anything, nothing that's interfering with my normal life, but I just need . . . well, I suppose I need to be sure.'

'And what exactly is it you want me to do, Richard?' I noticed the careful use of 'Richard'. She was alert, this woman. Alert and remarkably perceptive.

'Those hypnosis sessions that we had – I can't forget how much good they seemed to do me, how well I felt afterwards. I wondered . . . well, I wondered if you might consider seeing me privately and . . . trying it again.'

Emma was silent a moment, thinking the proposition over.

'Is Rick with you now?' she asked suddenly. The question was gently put, its tone not remotely threatening, but it made me jump. She *knew*. Just as surely as I was aware of her, she was aware of me.

'Let me handle this,' I said to Richard. He was glad to.

'I don't know if he is or isn't with me,' I said, through Richard. 'That's what I want to find out.'

'Under hypnosis?'

'Well, it worked last time.'

She was silent again. Did she realise, I wondered, that she was talking to me directly now? Would she give me any sign? 'Don't worry,' I said quickly to Richard as I felt his concern mount, 'I'm not going to come out into the open except under hypnosis.'

'Richard,' she said eventually, 'you have to realise that putting you under hypnosis won't necessarily exorcise this fear. You may unconsciously be looking for a way only to keep these two parts of yourself, if that's what you feel they are, separate and therefore manageable. There may be better ways of approaching the problem at this stage – analysis, for example. I'm not myself a qualified psychoanalyst, but there are some excellent people I'd be happy to recommend you to. Roger Killanin, for example. You got on quite well with him, didn't you?'

'Don't panic,' I said as Richard's heartbeat quickened. 'She's just probing. You're perfectly safe, you've done and you're going to do nothing to suggest that you're "nuts".'

'I don't think I want to get into something like that,' Richard's words came out relaxed and self-assured under my direction. 'I'm sorry, Emma – Dr Todd – I'm probably wasting your time.'

Get up, I told him, show her you're ready to leave. He did so.

'Don't go, Richard,' she said, not rising herself. 'And you were right first time, it's Emma.'

'But you're probably right and I'm just being over-sensitive,' I said. 'After all, hypnosis isn't something to be played around with casually.'

'There's a couch behind you, by the wall,' she said. 'If you really want me to, I'll put you under, and we'll carry on this conversation then.'

'Bingo!' I said to him in secret triumph. 'What did I tell you?'

'Can I talk to Rick?'

Richard was in deep trance. He had slipped into it with an ease which had surprised me. After all, willing though he was to be rid of me, he was also still acutely aware of the

114

risks to his own reputation and future ambitions if it became known that he had volunteered for further psychiatric treatment. I had expected at least some unconscious resistance to the familiar ritual of candle flame and soothing words, but there had been none. He had slipped as easily into trance as a baby into well-fed sleep.

'I'm here, Emma,' I said, experiencing the same overwhelming sense of relief at being able to speak with her directly that I always did. To an outsider the difference would have been imperceptible: the same voice, pretty much the same use of words and the same vocal mannerisms. Only Emma would have known, truly known, that Richard had gone, and this was Rick.

'Were you there all along?'

'Yes, I was here.'

'So you heard my conversation with Richard.'

'Yes.'

'What do you think about him coming here to get rid of you?'

'As a matter of fact it was my idea.'

'Ah,' she said, as though she had known all along. 'Did you discuss it with Richard?'

'At some length. You have to understand something, Emma . . . by the way, is that recorder still off?'

'Yes.'

'And there's nobody else listening?'

'Absolutely nobody.'

'Do I have your word on that?'

'You can trust me.'

'I know I can, Emma, otherwise I wouldn't be here. I sensed right from the start that there was something special about you. And I think you knew all along that I was real, didn't you?' I realised that was putting her on the spot, but I didn't have time to waste.

'I've always accepted you on your own terms, Rick,' was the reply she came up with. Circumspect. A little more on the fence than I'd have liked. But acceptable. She had her professional objectivity to maintain. It raised no barriers between us.

'You have to understand, Emma, that the story I originally told you in our first session was the literal truth. I do come from another universe, a parallel universe almost identical to this – but not quite. I did have a wife who died in an accident, and I do have a small son who needs me – and God knows I need him! That last "cure" was all a pretence. I thought maybe you'd guessed that at the time. I pretended to be "cured", but really I only went into hiding.'

'Why did you do that?'

'For Richard's sake, of course. He wasn't able to handle it then. But he's much stronger now.'

She paused a moment, thinking about her next question. 'Tell me,' she said eventually, 'just how much does Richard really know about you? Does he know everything that you've told me, or does he just have this sort of vague feeling that he was talking about when he came in here?'

'He knows everything. The trouble is, he doesn't feel comfortable about coming into the open about it. I'm sure you can understand that.'

'But surely he knew that as soon as he went into trance you were going to tell me everything.'

'Absolutely. But he'd rather I did it than him. He doesn't feel as comfortable with you as I do. After all, he was never privy to our relationship, yours and mine, when he was in trance before. He never heard how we talked, how each of us was able to read between the lines of what the other said. So I made an agreement with him, which was that he would come here – after all I couldn't come without him – and I would ask you for your help to leave him. But it's very important before we go any further that you understand that Richard is no more crazy than I am an hallucination. I'm depending on you to do everything you can to protect his reputation as a sane, normal – and by the way very decent – human being.'

'Richard will be totally protected under the doctor-patient

relationship. You have nothing to worry about on that score.'

'That's good to know. Thank you, Emma. Because I feel considerable responsibility for him. He's already been hospitalised because of me. And other things have happened.'

'What kind of other things?'

'Personal things – I'd rather not talk about them.'

'Do they concern his personal relationships?'

'Well, yes, as a matter of fact. So you understand I really have no right to discuss them.'

She understood, of course, and told me so. 'But how is it,' she went on, 'that you think I can help you to leave Richard and get back to your own life in this other universe?'

'By hypnosis.'

'And how will that work?'

'I've been thinking about it, Emma. Let me tell you how I see it, then you tell me if I'm right or not. I'm sure it must at least be worth a serious try.'

'Go on.'

'So far you've only ever hypnotised Richard. You've never hypnotised me. Right?'

'That's right. I've always hypnotised Richard.'

'Well, this time I want you to try to hypnotise me.'

'I see. Tell me, Rick, do you remember me saying one time that some people can't be hypnotised? That for some reason or another they're just immune?'

'I remember.'

'What makes you think you might not be one of those? After all, you were the one I tried to hypnotise in the first place, but it only worked on Richard.'

'But if you think about it, the person you were really trying to hypnotise was the one who was physically in the room with you – and that was Richard, even though you were calling him Rick at that time.'

'I suppose that's true.'

'Anyway, we won't know if I'm immune or not until you give it a try.'

She seemed to hesitate. I didn't know if it was from

117

reluctance or because she was thinking. 'You will try, won't you?' I asked, letting a note of anxiety creep into my use of Richard's voice.

'I'm just wondering about how I can do it. There are no prescribed techniques for hypnotising a person in your position.'

This didn't worry me. Her willingness was all that mattered. Once this was established, I knew she'd find a way. 'I'm just a layman,' I said, 'you're the expert. I'll bet you can do it.'

'Some people would say that you're already hypnotised. That when I hypnotised Richard I hypnotised you, too.'

'Anybody who believed that,' I said, a touch defensively, 'would have to believe that I was only part of Richard, and not who I say I am.'

I was relieved that she didn't pursue this line of argument. For an unnerving moment I had found myself suspecting the unthinkable: that she was only humouring me. Could I have been so wrong about her? But no. A moment later the conversation was back on course.

'All right,' she said, her soft voice once more firm with resolve, 'supposing I can find a way to hypnotise you, what do we do after that?'

'I want you to take me backwards in time, back through everything that's happened since I got here, then beyond that and into memories of my own life. I believe that if you can do that, if you can conjure up a sufficiently intense recollection of my own life, then I may have a chance of getting back to it.'

'At what point?'

'I guess at the point I left it.'

'A point which was so painful that you wanted nothing more in the world than to turn your back on it?'

'I think I'm ready for it now. I think I can handle it. And I have to try — for Charlie.'

'I don't know if it'll work, Rick.' It was a simple statement. There was no hint of disapproval, of judgment of any kind. Just a flat, scientific statement of fact. And it depressed me.

'But it's the kind of thing that's done under hypnosis all the time,' I protested. 'Regression!'

'Regression is a relatively rare technique.'

'But I'm always reading about witnesses to crimes who think they remember nothing, but under hypnosis can remember details like licence plates and other things they didn't know they knew.'

'That's not quite the same thing as regression.'

'But you're taking them back into their memories, making them relive them with the same vividness they first experienced them. That's all I'm saying. Make my memories of where I come from more vivid than my sense of being where I am! If you can do that, I honestly believe it might tip the balance – enough to put me back there.'

Another pause. Then: 'All right, I'll try. I have a hypnotic technique I use on blind patients, and as Richard's eyes are closed I'm going to try it on you.'

'You could have him open his eyes.'

'No, it's not the same. He sees, but you only sense what he sees. It's not the same thing as seeing.'

This woman was amazing. She understood everything. But then I thought of a logical objection.

'I don't hear things any more than I see them. All I can do is sense what he hears.'

'That's true,' she came back right away, 'but I don't think it's going to be an obstacle.' We were racing along at a fine clip now, a real team. 'The important thing,' she continued, 'is that I maintain a clear distinction between you and Richard by hypnotising you along different pathways. Anyway, like you said, we won't know unless we try.'

It began with a pulsating electronic sound on tape. I don't know what kind of speakers she was using, but they were good. Nor am I sure whether she was gradually increasing the volume or whether it was simply my attention that was growing more acute, but within a short time my whole consciousness was resonating with the sound. It was a kind of painless, ululating migraine that narcotised thought and blocked out everything except her voice. I was conscious of her careful rhythms, her measured cadences. They were similar to the ones she used on Richard; but this time I was feeling their seductive power from the inside, not just observing it with interested detachment. I began drifting into a strange limbo, stranger even than the one I had been living in for these past months. Already incorporeal, I became also mentally adrift, my willpower subsumed into some greater whole over which I had no control.

Suddenly I heard myself speaking. Or, more exactly, I heard a voice, Richard's voice, speaking for me. She had asked me a question and the voice was answering. It was answering honestly, speaking thoughts that came from me, yet I didn't understand how they were getting from me to the voice.

As I listened I heard a description of those first hours when I came to in the hospital following the accident. I began remembering things, one detail leading to another, with the voice trying to keep pace, but it couldn't. It fell silent, and I had a sudden, overwhelming sense that I was back there, bruised and half-drugged, drifting in and out of a bizarre fantasy that for a moment I had thought was real.

Then I heard Emma's voice again – clear, soft, totally commanding. She was taking me further back. Back into unconsciousness. Back into the darkness that separated there from here, then from now. And I knew with utter, terrifying certainty where I was going to come out.

Suddenly, just as my nerve failed, I sensed that I was not alone. I don't know how I knew. It wasn't knowledge of something at a distance, but an all-embracing certainty. Someone was addressing me. Not Emma. Not a voice of any kind. Another consciousness. Richard.

Richard, who was supposedly in trance, sidelined until Emma chose to wake him, had been observing all along, deceiving both of us.

'It's working,' he said. 'You're going back. That's what you wanted.'

'I'm scared,' I said. 'Oh, God, I'm so scared. It's too alone, I can't be this alone. Help me!'

Something in him snapped. A hidden rage burst forth like the blast of an exploding furnace, sending me tumbling and spinning into the long dark corridor that I had feared to enter.

'Let go of me, you parasite! I don't want you here! Let go!'

And suddenly, with a terrible certainty, I knew what was going to happen. I understood his willingness to brave ridicule by coming to Emma with a story that he knew would sound absurd. He didn't care about that any more.

'Richard,' I screamed, 'don't! Your anger! Don't! Don't give way to your anger!'

'It's none of your damned business!' he screamed back, his fury booming down the long, dark, slippery blackness. 'Get back to your own life, leave me to mine.'

'Don't destroy it!' I yelled back, not sure that he could hear through the roaring of his thoughts – those awful, bleak, vengeful and defeated thoughts. 'Don't buy the gun!'

The roaring stopped, switching instantaneously into an equally appalling, deafening silence.

It was still dark, but it was a different darkness. It was the darkness of my eyelids crushed together against the unendurable truth.

I opened them. My scream of grief and primitive defiance still echoed in the air, and my wife's blood lay thick and crimson on my hands.

Her eyes, in the tangled wreckage of her car, had the glazed permanence of death on them.

8

THE HANDS OF strangers drew me gently back. With quiet tact they turned me from the horror that transfixed me, paralysed my will, immobilised my limbs.

A woman was holding Charlie. His eyes were on me, unblinking and expectant. I wondered numbly what he wanted. To make it all right? To tell him not to be afraid, it was only a game? I felt a surge of anger at the cruelty of such an expectation, and at the same time stumbled forward and grasped him tightly in my arms. I clung to him for comfort and heard the sound of my own sobbing.

He knew now. He understood that it was not a game.

We moved together without moving. Decisions were suspended. Time and space curved around us into a closed mosaic of necessary events. I found that I was answering questions to a sympathetic cop: 'Hamilton. Yes, my wife. Anne. Middle initial E, for Elizabeth. Long Chimneys, Chapel Plains . . . Yes, if you would take us there . . . '

I realised that a police woman had taken Charlie and was holding him. She had removed her hat, revealing coarse blonde hair that fell forward, softening her face. She was talking to him, distracting him. She handed him back to me, but got with us into the car that was to take us home.

'Call . . . ? Oh, thank you, if you would. Please call . . . please call my lawyer, Harold Allison.'

I refused all medication. The fear of losing what fragile

grip on reality I had was greater than my need for comfort. I knew, and yet I didn't know, what was happening. 'It's shock,' I told myself. 'Don't talk, react. Answer questions. Yes. No. Would you? Thank you. You're very kind.'

Harold arrived, ashen-faced. I was sitting with a cup of herbal tea that someone had put into my hand. I must have held it out awkwardly, not knowing how to co-ordinate my movements, wanting to rise but for some reason being unable to. He took the cup away and sat with me. I think he held me for a moment, I'm not sure. I had lost all sense of being touched.

Or maybe it was just Harold's touch. Maybe a part of me that wasn't sure yet what was shock and what was memory had blocked out Harold's touch.

He took care of everything, of course, even calling an agency and finding a nurse for Charlie. Anne's parents would be coming from Maine for the funeral, but she had not been close to them and I would not have dreamed of asking them to take care of our son. My parents would not be coming from England for the funeral. My father was recovering from pneumonia, and my mother was reluctant to leave him. 'Yes, that's very thoughtful, thank you Harold – a nurse would be a good idea.'

How do you explain to a child that his whole world has changed? That in the span of a few seconds fate has denied him the right to be sure of anything ever again? How do you help a child make his peace with something that grown-ups still hide from?

Such questions for the moment pushed all else aside. My own bewilderment found its reflection in his and brought us close together. I debated briefly whether I should lie to him, but saw no way that it would help assuage his sense of loss. And I was certain that Anne would not have lied.

'You mean she isn't coming back?'

'No, Charlie.'

'Not ever?'

'Not in the same way. But in another way she'll always be

with us. In our hearts. If we listen very carefully, sometimes we'll be able to hear her there.'

He twisted his hands, rubbing the palms together and inspecting them with intense, abstracted concentration.

'Will she be able to hear us if we talk to her?'

'Yes, Charlie, I think she will.'

He was silent and very still. I could see there were tears in his eyes and he didn't know whether to fight them back or shed them. I put my arms out to him.

'Charlie, why don't you come and sit close with me for a while. Let's both try and listen for her, shall we?'

That night, when Charlie was finally asleep, I stretched out in a hot bath and tried to think. I knew one thing for sure: there was no one I could talk to. That way lay the Killanins and the private sanatoriums of this world as well as that.

I thought of Richard. What was happening to him now? Would I ever know?

In bed I browsed idly through a couple of newspapers. President Lloyd Bentsen had made an optimistic speech on his return from the Middle East. On an inside page a short paragraph announced that an obscure ex-actor called Ronald Reagan had died after a fall at a rest home in Burbank.

Flipping through television channels I watched the nation's favourite grandmother, Marilyn Monroe, duelling wittily with Carson on the 'Tonight Show' as they watched clips from her classic comedy series of the seventies. Struck by a sudden sense of guilt at being amused by such trivia on the day of my wife's death, I switched the television off.

But for me this was no longer truly the day of my wife's death. In my terms Anne – *my* Anne – had been dead for many weeks. I had been living with my sense of loss which, though irreparable, was now a fact of life. The pain was still there but, despite the shock of returning to the accident that morning, a layer of scar tissue was already in place.

The next few days passed in the formalised limbo of

bereavement: the funeral, the grief shared with relatives and friends, the condolences offered with awkward sincerity and accepted with muted thanks. I had asked that, in place of floral tributes, donations be made to Anne's housing trust, which I knew she would have wanted. The only flowers on her grave were two large wreaths from myself and her parents. I was touched by the size of the turn-out and, despite the fact that neither of us had been notably religious, by the few well chosen words delivered by our local minister.

I thought it better that Charlie did not attend the funeral. The nurse found for him by Harold was a godsend, taking up residence in one of our guest rooms and showing an extraordinary warmth and tact in all she did. Harold, too, was a tower of strength, there whenever I needed him and brushing aside all thanks.

But throughout it all my sense of isolation bore in on me until I felt almost suffocated. Ironically, it was even greater in this, my own world, than it had been in Richard's. Things once familiar had become strange. I found myself constantly comparing even the simplest of objects with its counterpart 'over there'. Was it the same or different? I was like a man who, through some accident or illness, has lost all sense of how to do things that the rest of the world take for granted, and now performs each task with a careful and unique deliberation.

During sleepless nights I asked myself if I could possibly have imagined everything that had happened since Anne's death. Could it be that others had been through the same experience? Had I merely suffered some rare but known reaction to extreme shock? Where the mind was concerned, anything was possible, but I did not believe it. I believed in my experience. And I wanted to talk about it.

Then one morning I awoke with a start from a restless doze, and realised that there was one person I could talk to. I rang him and proposed lunch at Chez Audran.

Tickelbakker sat across from me in a scene which uncannily mirrored the one I had so recently experienced in that other world. The only difference was that here he was talking with an old friend, not with a stranger. He was subdued out of respect for my bereavement, and my hesitancy in starting up a conversation did not seem as odd as it normally would have. He saw before him a man trying to cope with emotional devastation, seeking temporary escape in the abstract questions which had so often absorbed us in the past.

'Parallel worlds?' he said, seizing on the topic I had casually tossed out for discussion. 'It must be five years since I wrote that piece for *Particle/Wave*.'

'I just happened to pick it up last night,' I lied. 'Fascinating. Has anything happened to confirm or disprove the theory since you wrote about it?'

'On the contrary. They're even talking now about building a quantum computer that would do half its calculations in this universe and half in a parallel one simultaneously.'

'But a lot of people are still sceptical?' I suggested.

'Only because it's such a mind-boggling idea. But it's just as consistent with everything we know as it was twenty-five years ago.'

'In other words, every time a sub-atomic particle reacts with the system around it,' I said, rehearsing the argument with careful precision, 'whether in you or me, this table, in a rock on Mars, or on an asteroid in some hitherto undetected solar system way across the universe, then the whole of reality splits into a near-twin of itself – identical except for what that particular sub-atomic particle is doing.'

'There are good reasons for thinking that may be the case,' replied Tickelbakker, holding up his glass to examine the colour of the Vosne-Romanee '78 which had just been carefully poured into it.

'So that means,' I went on, 'that every single combination

of every sub-atomic particle in the universe that could happen actually does happen – somewhere.'

'Right.'

'Which means that every single combination of everything made up of these particles also happens – somewhere.'

'Mm-hm,' he nodded, swallowing reverently. The condition and temperature of the wine appeared to meet with his approval.

'So there are universes where Hitler won the second world war, America is still an English colony, and where – I don't know – pigs have wings. In fact where anything that could happen does happen.'

'Anything *possible*, but not anything *conceivable*.'

'I'm not sure I get that distinction.'

'The possibilities are limited by the laws of physics. There may be universes in which pigs have wings, but I doubt whether they would be aerodynamically very successful.' He gave me his toothy, boyish grin across the table, glad to feel that he was helping take my mind off the tragedy I had suffered.

'There's another thing I'd like to understand,' I said. 'I know these parallel universes are all wrapped up in supertime and superspace and don't run alongside each other like railway tracks, but what about the possibility of jumping from one to another? Could that ever be done?'

'Well, that's what they're talking about with this quantum computer. But so far it's only an idea.'

'But what about the possibility of, say, "me" in this universe getting across to another "me" in another universe?'

'That's a little tricky. You could make it work in science fiction, but not for real.'

'Why not?'

'If you, this you, wanted to enter a parallel universe and remain aware of what was happening, you'd first have to travel backwards in time in *this* universe to the point where the universe you want to get into branched off from this one.

127

And that,' he gave a dry little laugh, 'may be easier said than done.'

'But nobody rules out the possibility of time travel,' I persisted. 'You published a piece only a few months back. You said that both quantum theory and general relativity permit time travel in theory.'

'You've really been catching up on your reading, Rick. Heck, I think I could use a few sleepless nights myself.' Then, suddenly remembering the reason for my insomnia, he reddened and began mumbling a tremulous apology which I brushed aside impatiently.

'You wrote about "wormholes" in spacetime,' I went on. 'You described how one could be made. Two metal plates at each end of a tube. Shoot one of them through a loop at nearly the speed of light and return it to its original place, and you find that less time has elapsed at that end of the tunnel than the other. A time machine!'

'Theoretically possible. It only remains to solve the little practical problems – like shooting a metal plate through a loop at nearly the speed of light.'

'You know the one thing you scientists never consider?' I was growing excited now. I could hear my voice rising with an insistent, almost hectoring tone. 'You're always dreaming up these fancy machines that can travel at the speed of light, or operate in two realities at once, but you always overlook the most extraordinary machine of them all – one which we already have full use of!'

He looked at me curiously, not understanding what I was getting at.

'The human mind!' I said.

'I'm not sure I follow you.'

'You entirely overlook the possibility that all your complex maths, with its arrows of time pointing in two directions, and all your theories and thought experiments with their impossible-to-realise physical demands, may only be reflections of things that the human mind is already capable of doing by itself – without any outside help.'

'It's a point of view,' he commented a little drily, not wanting to argue with a man spouting nonsense as a consequence of emotional devastation.

'I'm serious,' I said. 'No one fully knows how the human brain works. We know that it's made up, like the rest of reality, of this mysterious wave/particle duality. It's the human brain itself that has started probing this duality – probing it, questioning it, striving to understand the very stuff of which it's made. Who is to say that what lives in this brain, this thing full of curiosity and invention that we call "the mind", or even "the soul", is not capable of making this leap from one universe to another? After all, there are references to Many Worlds in all kinds of ancient religions. It isn't just something dreamt up by modern science.'

'And how exactly would this mysterious mind mechanism work?'

'Maybe through drugs, maybe through meditation or hypnosis, or maybe sometimes through emotion.'

'Emotion? How d'you see that happening, Rick?'

'For instance, through grief and denial after some terrible emotional blow – the death of a loved one, for example. Maybe sometimes, in the right circumstances, this can create sufficient – whatever – energy to send at least some part of the self spinning across time-space into a parallel reality, a reality in which that loved one has *not* died . . . but where the price to be paid may be other changes that are as hard or even harder to bear.'

I realised he was staring at me, unblinking, his fork poised above his plate. I had said too much and was running the very danger, even with him, that had led to such trouble in the other world. I forced myself to lean back in my chair and give an easy grin.

'Hey, Mike, I know what you're thinking,' I said. 'It's written all over your face. Look, I'm just discussing possibilities, that's all. You're the one who's always saying keep an open mind. That's all I'm doing.'

129

'Sure, Rick, I know.' He lifted a forkful of aiguillettes de canard to his mouth and chewed it ruminatively. I had the feeling he wasn't enjoying it as much as usual.

9

MY LUNCH WITH Tickelbakker had been a mixed blessing. It had confirmed the reality of what had happened to me, but also underscored the unlikelihood of anyone ever believing it – even those, like Tickelbakker, best qualified to do so. It seemed as though everything conspired to increase my sense of isolation. I wondered how long my sanity could withstand the pressure.

In my dreams that night the two worlds mixed in surrealistic patterns. Anne was at the centre of them: a combination of my Anne and Richard's. I knew even before waking what these patterns meant: the spectre of jealousy that I had cruelly dangled before Richard was returning now to haunt me.

Charlie's nurse insisted on preparing breakfast for us both, although it was no part of her duties to do so. Her name was Peggy. She came from Kansas and was plump, well scrubbed, and with a broad, beaming face out of which shone pure good nature. My only regret was that, as she had warned me from the outset, she could stay only a few weeks before returning home to be married. But, as we sat around the table that morning, my thoughts were far from Charlie's ceaseless chatter, tuned though my ears were to listening for signs of distress or anxiety in him which I would do my best to deal with.

All I could think about was Anne: the difference between my dead Anne, and that other (presumably) still living one. And – God forgive me for even entertaining such a nightmare – the possible similarities.

I could not get the thought out of my head. If the genes which made up that identical twin were as near-perfect a copy as they had to be of the genes which had made up my Anne, then how many things could there have been about her – my Anne – that I never knew? By a slow, agonising process over which I had no control, my wife was becoming in retrospect a stranger to me. I began to imagine secrets, passions, lies and betrayals which in all likelihood had never happened, but which stained my memory of her like a slowly spreading poison. People around me imagined that my air of distraction was the result of my appalling loss. In truth it was suspicion.

She and Harold had always been close. I had been gratified by their friendship, taken its innocence for granted. Could I have been wrong? Could Harold's infinite concern for me in my sorrow be masking a secret, guilty sorrow of his own? It was the sort of question I could never put to him; an unthinkable accusation to make of a friend.

Anne's papers yielded no clue. No hidden cache of letters, no mysterious markings in her diaries, no tell-tale numbers on the records of her private phone line. I discovered that Balthazar's Motel existed in this universe exactly as it did in the other. I even went so far – I am ashamed to admit this – as to present Cy with separate photographs of Anne and Harold, tip him a hundred bucks, and ask him if he recognised either of them. He didn't.

Of course it could be that Harold had tipped him more to keep quiet. How could I know? How could I ever know?

How could I live without knowing?

Sometimes I think that when we describe something as 'unthinkable', what we mean is that we can't think about anything else. And when we dismiss a possible course of action as being 'out of the question', we mean that we've already decided to take it.

Harold's suggestion of a fishing weekend, just the two of us, had been tentatively put. He avoided phrases like 'do you good' and 'take your mind off things' – as, with his tactful, lawyer-ish nature, I would have expected. After satisfying myself that Charlie could safely be left with Peggy for a couple of days – indeed, I decided, it might be good for him to start becoming independent of me – we drove up early one Saturday morning to Harold's isolated lakeside cabin, as we had done so often before.

We took out his boat and caught fresh trout. Nothing much was said, but then it never had been on these weekends. We spoke if we had things to say, but our friendship was not the sort that made conversation a social obligation. Later, Harold cleaned and cooked the fish while I drove to the market and stocked up on bourbon, wine and beer.

By around ten that evening I was, in the metaphorical sense, feeling no pain. In a more literal sense, however, my anguish was unbearable.

'Harold,' I began, after a long silence broken only by the trickle of bourbon re-filling our two heavy glass beakers, 'there's something I have to say to you.' I paused for emphasis, regarding him solemnly from beneath knitted eyebrows. 'I know.'

He looked at me, uncomprehending. 'Know what?' he asked, his eyes round and unfocused with alcoholic, bleary innocence.

'You and Anne. I know.'

'Me and ... ? I don't know what you're ... I haven't the vaguest idea what you ... '

I was aware of my head swaying slightly above my hunched shoulders, elbows thrust forward on the table as I continued to fix him with a gimlet stare. I could see from the changing expressions on his face that he knew exactly what I was talking about.

His mouth worked for a few moments as though moulding the words into speakable shape.

'You can't be ... you can't be serious!'

'I'm not making a big deal. I'm not going to kill you. I'm not even blaming you. For all I know it was half her fault – if "fault" is the word. I just want you to tell me. Yourself. I need to hear it, Harold. You owe me that.'

'Rick, I ... I ... ' He sat back, his face white and his posture crumpling as though a fist had slammed him in the stomach. 'I can't believe what I'm hearing.'

'Let's do this without dramatics, evasions, or prevarications. Just get it over. Between the two of us.'

'Rick ... that is the most terrible thing I've heard in my life!'

'I didn't think it was so fucking great myself, if you want to know.'

'How can you possibly even ... even think of such a thing?'

I continued to stare at him, wondering how long he would squirm before confessing. 'Did you love her?' I asked, my head feeling heavy so that I had to make an effort to prevent it falling forward on the table. 'Or was it just sex?'

'Christ, Rick ... Oh, Christ ... I can't ... ' He pushed his chair back with a scraping noise. 'I can't ... I can't handle this ... I have to ... ' He struggled to his feet and started unsteadily for the door, like a drunk in urgent need of a bathroom.

I didn't move. I looked at my hand, still clenched around the bottle. I pulled it away, flexing the fingers slowly. If I was going to kill him, which I didn't mean to, I was going to do it with my bare hands and not with a weapon.

My own chair made the same scraping noise as his had, and then fell over with a clatter. The room swayed, but I steadied it by gripping the edge of the table. Then I started out into the night after him, pausing only to reach back for the bottle, which I wasn't going to hit him with but drink from.

The darkness and night air hit me like a wall and I almost fell over again, but the thought of the half-full bottle somehow galvanised my sense of balance and, after a moment's tricky footwork, I regained my equilibrium and pushed on after him.

I didn't find him at once. When I did, he was sitting on a rock, slumped forward with his head in his hands. I didn't think he'd heard me, but he must have, because he spoke my name.

'Rick ... Rick ... I don't know why you said that, but it's all right ... it's all right ... '

'What d'you fucking mean it's all right?' I roared. I hadn't meant to roar, but I could hear my voice filling the night. 'You fuck my wife – you, my so-called best friend! – and then *you* tell *me* it's all right!'

He didn't answer. He was making a funny kind of sound. Then I realised he was sobbing.

'Listen,' I said, quieter now, 'I told you I wasn't going to do anything about it. I just wanted ... I just wanted to know, that's all.'

We were silent for a while, him sitting there rocking, me swaying over him.

'Harold,' I began, my voice hoarse now, 'she's dead. It can't hurt her, but it's killing me. Tell me how it happened, how it started. Where? When?'

He looked up at me. My eyes had grown accustomed enough to the dark to see that his face was streaked with tears. He didn't speak, just shook his head slowly back and forth, back and forth. The motion made me dizzy. I lurched backwards, forwards, and then the ground came up hard and hit my knees. I continued to sway, but didn't fall any further. I just looked at him, kneeling, as though in prayer.

'I loved Anne,' he began, 'like I love you. Of course she was a beautiful woman. Of course I was aware of that. But I couldn't have. I couldn't!'

The words swirled around me, echoing in my head.

'Listen,' he went on, 'I'll tell you something. You want a confession? I'll give you a confession. I've had affairs. Not just the ones you know about. I've had affairs with married women. One of them almost wrecked my career – the wife of a client. I'm capable of being a bloody awful shit, and I can give you the names to prove it. D'you want the names?'

I started to shake my head, but the dizziness came back and I stopped.

'You can have them if you want them,' he said. 'All the names. I'll write them out. I'll sign them. But never Anne. I could never have done that. Nor could she. Believe me.'

I tried to speak. It wasn't easy. 'You're either a brilliant fucking actor,' I muttered through dry lips, 'or . . . ' I became aware of the alternative, arcing slowly through the air and exploding like a distant, muffled bombshell, 'or you're telling me the truth.'

'Of course I'm telling you the truth! You dumb great piece of shit! That's what I'm telling you!'

Suddenly I felt deflated and foolish, kneeling there, not knowing what to say or do. To fill the moment I held out the bottle for him to drink. I think it was a peace offering. He took it and flung it as far into the night as he could. I didn't hear it land.

'We've had enough. Both of us. I'm putting you to bed.'

'Yeah . . . okay . . . '

He helped me to my feet. By the time I got there I think I was helping him to stay upright as much as he was helping me. He looked at me, his face close to mine.

'What the hell made you say that?' he asked, his gaze moving back and forth between my eyes, trying to focus, trying to see into them.

'If I told you, you wouldn't believe me,' I said.

'Then let's forget it. It never happened. Come on.'

We stumbled towards the light inside the cabin.

I woke late to the smell of coffee and frying bacon. I don't know how I got to it, but I threw up from the window. A few minutes later, after pouring cold water on my head and rinsing my mouth, I faced Harold across the table we had been sitting at last night.

'How're you feeling?' he asked, looking none too well himself.

'Like a raw egg in a thin shell.'

'You'll feel better when you've eaten something.'

He put a plate in front of me, but my eyes stayed on him, looking for something. What? Resentment? Anger? I don't know.

'Harold,' I began, 'I remember what I said. And I want you to know that I'm sorry.'

'We agreed that we'd forget it,' he said, 'so let's do that. Now eat your breakfast, and let's go catch some fish.'

10

LOOKING BACK, I am convinced now that Harold must have sensed there was something more on my mind than just the pain, dreadful though it was, of my loss. He must have sensed a barrier growing between himself and me, and decided to provoke a confrontation that weekend by the lake to clear the air.

It had worked and I was grateful to him. I believed his denial. It had restored to me the memory of the Anne I loved and trusted, and wanted more than anything to go on loving.

Also, I found myself at last becoming free of the obsession to talk about and share the mystery of that split second between my arrival at the scene of Anne's death and my acceptance of it. I believed in what had happened to me. I believed that it was real.

But what is 'real'?

The question for now was of secondary importance. What mattered was life. My life, my son's life. Metaphysical speculation gave way to the problems of the day, like finding another nurse for Charlie before Peggy left, and doing something about the injection of money that my business sorely needed.

Before Anne's death, I had been so confident of the bank's backing that I simply hadn't thought in terms of alternatives. Harold had known they were going to offer me the money, and my own doubts and worries had not been serious. If I had been asked what would happen if the bank changed its mind, I would simply have said that we'd carry on the way we were. But things are never that simple.

Businesses, I was about to learn, either reach a plateau and die there, or they move on up to the next level. I had been on the point of making that move, and assumed that we would now pick up where we had left off. I had reckoned, however, without the innate conservatism of men in suits.

I was unaware of the whispering at first. It was Harold who told me what they were saying. They spoke to him as to the sensible member of the family, the one who could be relied on to avoid trouble, smooth things over, find ways out of situations which had become untenable.

'Look, Rick,' he began, clearly embarrassed by what he had to tell me, 'if you'd got a phone call at the bank saying that Anne had just been killed in an accident five miles away, you'd have been showered (a) with sympathy, and (b) with all the money you need.

'But the fact is that, well, the timetable of events that has emerged in retrospect has, I can only say, an "unusual" look to it.'

'What d'you mean?' I asked, not catching on at first.

'Rick you ran out of that meeting at the bank a full thirteen minutes before the accident happened.'

'Oh.' I was beginning to see.

'Exactly. And they've all picked up on that by now, and it bothers them.'

'Yes. I can see it might.'

Something was going on which did not sit easily on the ledgers and balance sheets of the financial world. I was no longer somebody with whom that world felt comfortable. I had become, although the term was never used openly, a 'freak'.

Harold did his best to argue with them that such things were not unknown to serious science. People who were very close sometimes shared levels of communication which defied all rational explanation. He cited cases from a stack of books on extra-sensory perception, but to no avail. The bank's mind, and vaults, were closed.

To be honest I didn't care that much. I was a natural optimist. If the business failed I would start over. The future to me had always been filled more with promise than with menace. Success, I believed, was generated by ideas, not by shuffling figures around on paper.

Harold, however, was worried. It was a good sign. I knew he would come up with something. Meanwhile I started interviewing nurses for Charlie.

The agency found by Harold and which had sent Peggy was highly efficient. I liked the first three girls they sent, but felt they weren't quite right for the position. Then one morning I got a call to say they were sending over a slightly more mature applicant whom they thought would be ideal. My heart stopped when I heard her name.

It was Emma Todd.

I opened the door and looked into clear blue, smiling eyes. Her car was parked in the drive behind her.

It *was* Emma. The same Emma. She looked younger. Her hair was a rich chestnut, falling nearly to her shoulders and framing her face in gentle contours. She wore little make-up, just enough to highlight those classic features which lit up with a smile of such warmth that I felt myself drawn down into it like a drowning man.

'Mr Hamilton?'

'Yes.' I cleared my throat. 'Miss Todd? Please come in.'

She moved with an easy, natural grace. Her clothes were simple and inexpensive, but chosen with an inherent sense of style. There was a freshness about her, a lightness in her every movement.

My voice seemed to come from somewhere else. It was high, not my voice. 'Won't you sit down?'

'Thank you.'

She looked up at me. I must have seemed strange, tongue-tied and awkward. 'Can I get you . . . I was just . . . I have some coffee . . . '

I put the tray in front of her, clumsily pushing aside books and newspapers. She took it black with no sugar. The ritual of pouring gave me precious moments to collect my wits. I could not believe that this was actually happening. But it was.

'I assume the agency sent you my references,' she said, taking the cup from my unsteady hand.

'Oh . . . yes . . . they seem fine.' In fact they were more than fine. She had been two years with the family of a high-ranking British Embassy official in Washington. I was a little surprised to find her prepared to take on such a relatively modest job as the one I was offering, and told her so.

'My parents live close by,' she told me. 'I'd like to be nearer to them than I have been.'

It answered one question, but left many more. Why was this beautiful woman unmarried, without children, without a more ambitious career? Why was she not blind? Why was the blind Emma Todd a psychiatrist and this one a children's nurse?

My head was full of questions that would have to wait. My only fear was that she wouldn't take the job and that I would never get around to finding out the answers.

'It seems to me the most important thing,' I said, sitting opposite her, 'is that you meet Charlie. He's just over the road. I'll call him.' I got to my feet again, using the restless movement to cover my nervousness, and picked up the phone.

Charlie adored her from the moment they met, and Emma clearly felt the same way about him. Within a week she was installed in the house. I couldn't believe my luck.

I knew I was in love with her. That much I didn't even have to ask myself. I was an irretrievably lost cause. I was also consumed with guilt at the thought of this happening so soon after Anne's death. It was ironic that my recent fears about her loyalty should be so quickly followed by my own betrayal of her memory.

And yet I didn't feel that it was a betrayal. I still loved Anne as I always had. If she were alive, Emma would be no threat to that love.

But Anne wasn't alive, and Emma was. Also Emma and I had a history, a unique relationship – even if I was the only one of us aware of it.

It was clear to me that I must say or do nothing to betray my feelings for the time being. In a way that was an advantage. Emma and I could get to know each other, becoming friends before we became lovers, as we surely must.

The thought that there might be any obstacle in that idyllic path did not at first occur to me. When it did, only hours after that first meeting at which she had agreed to take the job, I was pitched into a turmoil of anxiety.

Suppose there was another man? There had to be – a woman like that.

And yet she obviously lived alone, or else she would not have been free to take the job of full-time live-in nurse.

Could she be gay? It was a possibility, of course. But even if she was, she obviously had no firm commitments. Perhaps in time . . .

But I was getting way ahead of myself. I forced myself to calm down. It wasn't easy. I did something I have rarely done. I had a large Scotch at eleven in the morning.

The first month of Emma's stay in the house was both torture and delight. Torture because of the stranglehold I had to keep on my emotions, and a delight just because she was there.

At least I got to know her as I hoped I would. She was neither married, gay, nor in love with anyone else. She had been married once – at age nineteen, to a soldier. He was obviously a high-flyer, some years older than her and probably destined for the General Staff. She had adored him and had given up all thought of a career of her own to follow him on his postings. They had one child, William, who had been killed, aged five, by a hit-and-run driver in Germany. The driver had never been found.

In the way these things sometimes happen, the marriage had not survived the tragedy. Neither of them became involved with anyone else, but the special thing that had existed between them had gone. She was twenty-seven when they divorced.

She had done her best to pick up the threads of her life, but it was too late to realise fully the dreams of her youth. She had wanted once to be a doctor. She had done well at school and had been told it was a possibility. Now she settled for nursing training. The institutional life of hospital work had not suited her, but she had stuck with it for a couple of years. During that time she had an affair with a doctor. Then she had fallen ill with weakness and headaches.

The condition had turned out to be a viral infection which was quickly cured. However, in the course of diagnosis a rare genetic condition had been found. It in no way threatened her health or well-being, but meant that there was a 50 per cent danger that any future child she might have would be born blind, as Emma's brother had been. No one had suspected the reason until Emma's diagnosis.

Her relationship with the doctor had ended, because they had been talking of marriage and having children, but she refused now to take that risk. She had left hospital work and become a children's nurse.

That was her story to date. She adored children and was not unhappy. She did not think she would marry again.

'Oh, Emma, how wrong you are,' I said to myself, imagining the day, maybe ten months, a year in the future, when I would be able to say it openly to her.

I was proud of the fact that she had talked to me so freely, and encouraged by it. Clearly she trusted me. The fact that I made not even the most indirect of advances to her during those first weeks that she was in the house had given her confidence.

Of course there was talk among the neighbours, and she

was as aware of it as I was. But we laughed it off and rose above such narrow-mindedness.

'But we'll give them something to talk about in time,' I promised myself. 'Just you wait and see, my darling Emma. Just you wait and see.'

Harold had redoubled his efforts to find the investment we needed, but without success.

I remained convinced in my old-fashioned way that stability, not growth, was the first law of business. Of course I didn't know what I was talking about, which only made me more determined to prove myself right.

Strictly speaking, we grew a bit. We added one new title to our list: the specialist journal for demographers that we had been talking about for some months. It was hardly a new plateau, but it was the sort of growth I felt comfortable with.

Inevitably the launching of a new title meant a good deal of extra work, but I was glad of that. It was a distraction from my loss – and from my new unspoken love.

Travelling also helped, and I had to do a lot. It felt good to be able to leave Charlie with the woman who would one day soon become his stepmother.

As the days and weeks passed, although still nothing had been said, I became increasingly convinced that Emma felt as I did. I sensed that same complicity growing between us that had existed in the other life. Sometimes I almost felt that, by some strange intuition, she already knew the whole story. But maybe that was wishful thinking.

The question of how much I should ultimately tell her became my main preoccupation. How much of my story would I share with the woman who was to share the rest of my life?

Would I take the risk – even though I was convinced in Emma's case it was an almost non-existent risk – of having her think I was insane?

I turned the problem over in my mind as I flew back from a four-day trip to the west coast, where I had gone to sign up a UCLA psephologist as a regular contributor to the new journal. I would have to tell her something. Perhaps a hint before marriage, and the rest later.

Harold had insisted on meeting me at the airport. I quickly spotted him in the small crowd awaiting the flight, but as I approached I was surprised to see that Emma was with him. Instinctively I looked for Charlie, too, even though it was way past his bedtime. Then I realised that Emma's presence there probably meant he was staying over with a friend. I was happy to see her and touched that she'd made the effort.

I kissed her there at the arrivals' gate for the first time. Lightly on the cheek. She gave me a hug. Harold's being there made it all right. An affectionate but still innocent greeting.

But it set a precedent. A barrier had been breached. From now on physical contact between us would no longer be taboo.

On the drive from the airport Emma sat in front with Harold, leaving me room to spread out in the back. Harold, knowing that I never ate on planes, had booked a table at Chez Arnaud for a light supper. Emma confirmed my assumption that Charlie was staying over with friends. I suddenly realised with a shiver of excitement that she and I would be returning to an empty house together.

Harold ordered champagne while we looked over the menu. It was after we'd ordered that he dropped his bombshell.

'Naturally we wanted you to be the first to know, Rick,' he began. 'You've been so busy these last couple of months that you probably haven't even realised how much Emma and I have been seeing of each other. Anyway the fact is that I've asked her to marry me and, well, I'm very happy and proud to tell you she's accepted.'

I was speechless. I looked from him to her. She was gazing

at him with a glow of love in her eyes. He was looking at her the same way. I might as well have not been there. I felt like, and was, an irrelevance. Excess baggage that would be got rid of as soon as was convenient.

Obediently doing what was expected of me, I raised my glass and offered them my deepest and sincerest good wishes for their future together.

But inside I was screaming.

11

THEY DROVE BY the house to drop me off. Emma was spending the night with Harold. She said she would collect Charlie from his friend's house on her way back in the morning.

I don't know how I had got through supper without betraying my feelings. Fortunately they put down the deadness in my voice and face to tiredness. And anyway they were too wrapped up in each other to pay me much attention. No wonder she could afford to kiss me now. She did it again when I got out of the car. Kissed me like a friend, an uncle, a member of the family you run into at weddings but otherwise never think about.

Almost the worst part was how I'd deceived myself into thinking that there was something between us. Had I become so totally out of touch with reality? Could I trust my judgment about anything any more?

That night, exhausted though I was, I didn't go to sleep for many hours. I wandered from room to room with a compulsive restlessness. I drank but didn't get drunk. At least I didn't feel that I was getting drunk, just blurring the stark fact of my humiliation.

I thought of them in Harold's bed. A kaleidoscope of pumping, lusting images of erotically charged flesh swirled through my imagination. As the night wore on I became convinced that they both must have known of my feelings towards Emma. It isn't possible to hide something like that, and I was foolish to have thought I could.

There was no other explanation of their behaviour —

meeting me at the airport and sitting me down at Chez Arnaud before I even had time to be five minutes alone with her. They meant to present me with a *fait accompli* to forestall the embarrassment of any declaration on my part, which they must have sensed was drawing near. I could hear them now, laughing. 'Did you see his face? I thought he was going to burst!'

Or, even worse, pitying. 'Poor Rick, let's hope he isn't too hurt. But it was best to get it over with.'

And so I went on, prowling endlessly from room to room, a bottle in one hand and a glass in the other, the whole house ablaze with lights.

I don't know when or where I fell asleep, but suddenly I became aware that I was dreaming. Somebody was trying to tell me something, but I couldn't understand what. A bunch of papers were put into my hand. I knew that they carried the same information I had been straining to hear, but I couldn't read the print. The harder I tried, the blanker the paper became.

'I'm dreaming,' I told myself. 'I'm angry and frustrated because I'm trying to understand something, and I can't.' I threw the papers down, refusing to be made a fool of.

Then I saw where I was.

I was in Richard A. Hamilton's luxurious drawing room. It was night and the man who had just been speaking to me was stocky, with an expressionless face and eyes that were set too close together. He made me think of a bouncer at the door of some low dive, but I knew that in fact he was a private detective. I don't know how I knew that, but I did.

With a terrible finality I also knew that something he had said had just signed Anne's and Harold's death warrants. I looked down.

The blank white sheets of paper on the carpet were no longer blank. They were covered now with closely printed paragraphs. Without reading them I knew that they gave dates and places, times and telephone numbers, credit card bills and plane reservations. He had done a thorough job, this stocky little man.

There were also, I could see now, photographs, their edges pointing out between the printed pages. I didn't want to look at them, because I had already seen them. I knew what was in them. Those pitilessly literal images of Harold and Anne danced with my nightmare imaginings of Harold and Emma. My hands flew to my face, uselessly covering my eyes against what was already seared into my brain.

The stocky man was saying something. I had to silence the gasping noises coming from my throat to hear him.

'It's up to you. You just have to say the word, Mr Hamilton.'

'I'm sorry?' I mumbled. 'What did you say?'

'Anything you want taking care of, Mr Hamilton. I mean *anything*. A private arrangement between you and me.'

I understood what he was offering, and shook my head. 'No,' I said. 'I'll take care of it myself. Just tell me how much I owe you.'

He shrugged as though to take a life, two lives, or not take them was all the same to him. He named a figure and I crossed to a table where my cheque-book lay open. I took out a pen, filled in the cheque, and signed it Richard A. Hamilton.

'Thank you, Mr Hamilton,' he said as I handed it to him. 'And remember, if you change your mind, the offer's good.'

He left me alone in the middle of the room and saw himself out. I waited until I heard the front door close, then I went into my study.

I knew exactly what I was going to do. I knew where I had hidden the key to open the drawer in which was kept the gun that I had bought ten days earlier. I loaded it exactly as I had been shown, and slipped it into my pocket.

As though in a dream, I left the apartment and took the lift to the garage.

As though in a dream?

I knew exactly where I was going. I drove calmly, carefully, totally in control. The awful finality of what lay ahead caused me no concern.

After all, it was only a dream.

All I had to do was play the role set out for me. Events carried me forward without effort. I did not know the building that I parked outside, yet I knew that the address had been provided by the stocky man.

I did not know why I took the elevator to the seventh floor, or how I knew to turn left and follow the corridor until I reached apartment 7b.

It was only as I stood outside it that I remembered a key I had been given by the stocky man. I took it from my pocket and slipped it silently into the lock. It fitted perfectly. In my other hand I had the gun.

The living room was empty, but there was a glow of light from the bedroom. And voices.

They looked up at me from where they lay, naked, astounded, their faces full of fear.

I did not pull the trigger. The double explosion was just another thing that happened in the dream. It must have come from somewhere else. A car backfiring outside. A window banging in the night.

Can dreams contain noises like that?

Surely not.

12

AND NOW I sit in prison awaiting trial. I am writing this for
you, Dr Todd. Emma.

I want you to believe that I am sane. I have told my
lawyers that I will not contemplate any plea that attempts
to use insanity as an excuse for what I have done. That is
a final and unalterable decision.

It's true I had a breakdown for which you treated me.
It's also true that I had a relapse after learning of my wife's
affair with my best friend. My symptoms were exactly as I
have described them in this document: the irrational conviction that I came from another parallel reality and that I was
only temporarily inhabiting the mind and body of Richard
A. Hamilton.

But I accept now that this was a delusion. There is
no such thing as a parallel universe or alternative reality.

Yes, the idea exists on a theoretical level, but it has no
meaning for our daily lives, our real lives. I am Richard
A. Hamilton and I live in this world. Jack Kennedy died
in 1963, when I was a child. Marilyn is also dead. There
has been much speculation that the two events were not
unconnected. I don't know about that. It doesn't concern
me. I'm only trying to show you that I know what world
I'm living in.

Lyndon Johnson became president after Jack Kennedy.
Bobby was never president because he was murdered by
someone called Sirhan Sirhan. Then there was Nixon and,
after Watergate, Gerald Ford. Then Jimmy Carter, Ronald

Reagan, and George Bush. Lloyd Bentsen was Mike Dukakis's running mate in '88.

You see, we live in the same world. You're a psychiatrist and I'm in real estate. I'm going to ask if I can get this document translated into braille, because I'd rather you read it yourself than have anybody read it to you.

I guess – this is embarrassing and a little silly, but I'm going to say it anyway – I guess I am a little in love with you, Emma. But then I would be, wouldn't I? Isn't it called 'transference'? You became very important to me during my recovery from my breakdown.

Above all I don't want you to feel guilty for not having prevented what happened. There was nothing you could have done that might have stopped me killing Anne and Harold. The hurt and anger went too deep. Such things are primaeval. Reason and science have no power over them.

So forgive me, Emma, for being one of your failures. You got rid of my delusions and restored me to sanity.

Unfortunately I turned out to be more dangerous sane than crazy. But now I'm ready to pay the price.

It's all there is left.

PART TWO

Mr Kenneth J. Schiff
Bronstein, Schiff & Hartman
Attorneys at Law

Dear Mr Schiff,

You will by now have read your client's account, written at my request, of his 'experiences' leading up to the double murder with which he stands charged. I would like to add this note of comment.

I first interviewed Mr Hamilton (hereafter 'the patient') at the Beatrice Davenport Memorial Hospital, where he had been admitted following an automobile accident. Although not seriously injured physically, he was manifesting symptoms of severe and persistent delusion – namely the disappearance of an imaginary child.

On that occasion I formed no opinion as to whether this delusion was organic or otherwise in origin. Before I could interview him further, he had absconded from the hospital and been taken into police custody. Although released into the care of his wife, he was later admitted to the Dodge-Kesselring Psychiatric Clinic and placed under the supervision of my colleague, Dr Roger Killanin.

Four days after his admission, Dr Killanin invited me to interview him once again at the clinic. At Dr Killanin's suggestion, I informed the patient that I had personally taken the initiative in asking to see him. This was because the patient was exhibiting an irrational hostility towards both Dr Killanin and the clinic, which was making treatment difficult.

I found the patient lucid, although agitated, and manifesting elements of delusional paranoia. My reasons for suggesting hypnosis were twofold:

First, I felt that the further use of drugs could only be deleterious to the patient's stability and willingness to co-operate.

Second, in view of the detailed nature of the patient's delusions, I suspected some form of cryptomnesia, the origins of which were more likely to be uncovered by hypnosis than by other means.

The patient proved to be an excellent hypnotic subject. Using a standard induction technique, I was able to induce a medium deep trance without difficulty. Over the following three weeks, I conducted a total of seven sessions with the patient, inducing on each occasion a slightly deeper trance. At the end of this time, it was clear to me that the delusional phase of the patient's illness was currently inactive. However, I remained concerned that I had uncovered no causal factor for the specific nature of the delusion. None the less, it was decided to allow the patient to return home.

Several weeks later, I received a call from him at my private office. He asked to come and see me. You have read the patient's account of that interview and the ensuing session of hypnosis. At the end of the session he thanked me for my help and left. Although I suggested at least one follow-up consultation, the patient did not consider this necessary and declined to co-operate.

It was some three months after this that the patient committed the double murder of his wife and her lover. You inform me that the patient had been aware of the affair for some time, and had apparently hoped that it would run its course. You say he had bugged the motel room where they were meeting; then, when they had changed venue and also begun taking trips away together, he had hired a private detective agency to detail their movements.

These acts, in and of themselves and without reference to their surrounding circumstances, do not necessarily indicate a paranoid state of mind. In this particular case, the patient's acts would seem, to some extent, justified and therefore rational. We must be careful about the strategy we attempt to use in his defence.

The precise circumstances leading up to his final violent act are, you say, not known. It is clear, however, that the patient made no attempt to conceal his crime or evade arrest, and was still on the scene with the murder weapon in his hand when the police arrived.

On the first occasion I interviewed him in prison; he was sullen and uncommunicative, exhibiting marked suicidal tendencies. When I asked him whether the murders had been committed by 'Rick' or 'Richard', he once again said that 'Rick' did not exist and never had existed. When I reminded him of his earlier conviction to the contrary, he insisted that he had been cured of this delusion since our last hypnosis session.

He stated emphatically that he wished to take full responsibility for what he had done, adding that his only regret was that the crime had not been committed in a state where capital punishment was practised.

I told him that if he did not want my help in establishing a defence against a charge of murder, then he was not obliged to accept it. However, I informed him that there was something he could do for me which would be valuable in my work in general, not just with reference to himself. I told him that I would like him to write an account – from the perspective of his currently normalised condition – of the experience of being two persons in one.

After brief consideration, he agreed. Five days later, the document you have read was completed.

As you will see, the patient begins his narrative in the 'parallel' reality, in which his wife supposedly dies in a car accident, and ends it in this reality, in which he kills her. It does not require special training to recognise here the mechanism of guilt and denial at work on an unconscious level. Nor is it difficult to see in the figure of the child, as in the whole idyllic picture of the 'other' marriage, the elements of wish-fulfilment fantasy.

You will also have observed the dual role which I myself play in this narrative. I do not propose here to analyse this duality beyond noting that it is consistent with the common phenomenon of transference between patient and physician.

I believe that it would be possible to construct a defence to the charge of first degree murder on the grounds of the patient's mental condition. However, the question of whether or not he is fit to stand trial is more difficult to establish, and I will give you my opinion on that after my next visit to him.

Yours sincerely,

Emma J. Todd, M.D.

Dr Roger Killanin
Dodge-Kesselring Clinic
Castle Heights

Dear Roger,

A delicate matter has arisen on which I would value your advice. It comes out of my visit to Richard Hamilton this morning to discuss the document of which you have a copy.

I found him significantly altered in mood. He was positive, relaxed, and seemingly self-confident. The first thing he said was that he hoped I hadn't been embarrassed by what he had written about me. I assured him that he should not worry on that score.

He said he had found that writing the account had been a therapeutic experience, adding that he suspected that had been my real reason for asking him to do it. I conceded that it was certainly one reason.

At this point he asked me if I had my tape recorder with me. I told him I had, and he asked me to switch it on. The following is a transcript of our conversation:

Transcript From Tape

PATIENT: I think it may be useful for you to have this for reference later. We have nothing to hide any more.

DR TODD: 'We'?

PATIENT: Richard and I. Or, if you prefer, Rick and I. Let's not quibble about the billing. We are as one now. Which is not the same thing, you understand, as being one. Frankly, the importance of writing our story down didn't strike either of us as being quite as enormous as it was until after we'd finished and sent it off to you. That accounts for the downbeat ending. We're both feeling a lot more positive now.

DR TODD: I can see that. Tell me, am I speaking with both of you at the moment? Or just with one of you?

PATIENT: You're speaking with both of us. We find we can listen, think, consult, and come up with a mutually agreed response so fast that nobody is aware of any delay at all. It's Richard's voice, of course. That's because Rick's voice, like the rest of his body, is back where he left it, in the other universe looking after Charlie.

DR TODD: Okay, but let me understand this. If Rick is still back in the other universe, what is the part of him that's here now?

PATIENT: We don't know. While he's here it feels like it's the whole of him. But that can't be so, because it's not his body, it's Richard's body. And the experiences he is having are Richard's experiences. They're comparable to his own, but not the same.

DR TODD: I see.

PATIENT: No you don't. (Laughter) You think you're talk- ing to a crazy guy. It's okay – you've been great, Emma. Can we ask you just one last favour?

DR TODD: What's that?

PATIENT: Rick has to go back. He can't do it without you.

DR TODD: What are you asking me to do?

PATIENT: Let's just review what we know, Emma. We know that Rick can jump between two universes. Maybe in time more than two, but for now let's stick with what we've got. The first time he did it by accident, the second time by intention, under hypnosis. That second time he arrived back at exactly the point of his departure – which was what he wanted. And this last time he dreamed himself here.

DR TODD: Has he tried dreaming himself back?

PATIENT: As a matter of fact he has. And d'you know what? He can do it. Or at least he could if he wanted. He dreamed himself back and almost woke up once. But he doesn't want to do that. He doesn't want to go back to exactly the point where he left. We have something more ambitious in mind. You want to know what that is?

DR TODD: Of course I do.

PATIENT: Time travel.

DR TODD: Time travel?

PATIENT: It's the only way to clear up this mess, Emma. We've talked about it and we really believe it'll work.

DR TODD: Would you like to explain how?

PATIENT: Emma, you've read what we wrote about Rick coming over here, and how all that thing happened. You remember it pretty well, don't you?

DR TODD: I do.

PATIENT: So you remember how it all started – Rick having all those strange feelings, waking up in the night, almost killing himself in his car, passing out, finally getting this premonition that Anne was in danger. Don't you realise what the explanation of all that is?

DR TODD: Why don't you tell me?

PATIENT: Rick was reaching back in time – from here! – and trying to warn himself what was going to happen. Only he didn't make it. It all happened anyway.

DR TODD: I see.

PATIENT: Do you, Emma? Do you really? We'd both really like to believe that.

DR TODD: I understand perfectly what you're saying.

PATIENT: But do you understand what we have to do now?

DR TODD: Tell me.

PATIENT: We have to try again, Emma! Put Rick back under hypnosis and get it right this time.

DR TODD: I'm not sure I can do that.

PATIENT: You can do it, Emma. We've figured it out. All you have to do is put him –

DR TODD: I mean I'm not sure I can administer hypnosis – here.

PATIENT: What's the problem?

DR TODD: This is a prison. I'm not free to behave here as I would in my own office, or in a hospital room.

I'm constrained by certain legal obligations here.
We both are.

End of Transcript

So that, Roger, is my problem. What do you think I should
do?

As ever,

Emma

Director: Roger A. Killanin

Mr Raymond P. Garrison
Office of District Attorney

Dear Mr Garrison,

The shocking death in custody of Richard A. Hamilton clearly requires the most scrupulous investigation. However, I feel that neither truth nor clarity is well served by the current tendency both in professional and media circles to make a scapegoat out of my colleague, Dr Emma Todd.

I would like to make it absolutely clear that, before undertaking the course of action which led to this unfortunate event, Dr Todd went to considerable lengths to ensure that her action was both legally and professionally justified. I strongly oppose any suggestion of improper conduct on her part, and have every confidence that the upcoming inquiry will exonerate her.

You have seen a copy of the letter in which Dr Todd asked my advice before agreeing to her patient's request for further hypnotic treatment. I in turn spoke by telephone to the State Correctional Board and to the President of the State Psychiatric Association before passing on their advice to her.

I was informed that Dr Todd would be in violation of

neither law nor ethical propriety if she administered to the patient any treatment she saw fit in order to establish his unfitness to plead. The patient's stated desire to stand trial on the criminal charges brought against him, without any mitigating pleas on the grounds of his mental health, in no way compromised her right or duty as his physician, in co-operation with his lawyers, to establish such grounds if possible.

The clinical justification for this treatment was unchanged from the previous occasion. It seemed plain to both Dr Todd and myself that the patient was exhibiting, by this roundabout means, a willingness to seek out and confront the root cause of his delusion. It was our duty to encourage, not discourage, such an intention.

The session took place in an interview room in the prison. Only the patient and Dr Todd were present, though guards and a trained nurse had been posted outside to be called upon if necessary.

Trance was induced by a standard technique and with no resort this time to a secondary trance. Only 'Rick', however, was to be regressed, while 'Richard' was to remain in light trance.

The patient and Dr Todd agreed upon a self-reporting technique, whereby he would automatically report the depth of his trance on a scale from zero (normal consciousness) to fifty (plenary trance) whenever Dr Todd requested.

The following is an excerpt from the tape of the session.

Transcript From Tape

'RICK':   45 . . . I'm now at 45 . . .

'RICHARD':   I'm at 10, Emma. This is Richard. I can see Rick way down there. He's way ahead of me.

DR TODD: What can you see from where you are, Rick?

'RICK':   I can see where I have to go . . .

DR TODD: Where is that, Rick?

165

'RICK':	Further back . . .
DR TODD:	What is there further back?
'RICK':	Him . . . me . . . it's myself, but it's him . . .
DR TODD:	What is he doing?
'RICK':	He's dreaming. He's having some . . . (the patient laughs slightly here) . . . he's having some pretty sexy dreams there . . . Oh, wow, he'd really like to remember those dreams, but he's not going to . . . no, he's definitely not going to . . .
DR TODD:	Why not?
'RICK':	Because he's anxious about tomorrow, but does not want to admit it, and that's making him restless . . . He's coming up now . . . he's coming towards me . . .
DR TODD:	Can he see you?
'RICK':	I don't . . . no [know?] . . . no, he's gone right through me, like I was a ghost . . .
'RICHARD':	Emma, he's got to go further back . . .
DR TODD:	That's all right.
'RICHARD':	I'm still at 10, Emma. I can see him down there, but I can't help him.
DR TODD:	Give me your depth, Rick.
'RICK':	I'm at . . . almost . . . 50 . . .
'RICHARD':	Go! Go, Rick! Go!

NOTE: The patient's voice as 'Rick' is now weakened as though by strenuous physical effort, while 'Richard' remains vigorous and full of energy. There is no difficulty on the tape in telling which is speaking.

166

'RICK':   I must . . . I must . . .

DR TODD: It's all right, Rick, go back as far as you need.

'RICK':   I'm . . . I'm afraid . . .

DR TODD: There's no need to be afraid, Rick. What's your depth now?

'RICK':   I'm at 57 . . . it's still not far enough . . . Emma . . .

DR TODD: It's all right, Rick, you can go on back without deepening your trance. You're deep enough now to go back as far as you need. You don't have to go down any further, just go back. Can you do that?

'RICK':   Yes, I think . . . I think I . . .

'RICHARD': I've got to help him, Emma. He can't do this by himself.

DR TODD: I don't think that's necessary, Richard.

'RICHARD': I have to. He needs help. Rick, Rick . . .

DR TODD: All right, Richard, let's take you down slowly, calmly . . .

'RICHARD': There's no time for that. Oh, my God, look what's happening! I've got to get there!

DR TODD: Rick – give me your depth, Rick [No response]. Rick, give me your depth.

'RICHARD': It's no use, Emma. He's too far gone. Rick. Wait for me. Hold on. Wait for me.

DR TODD: Rick! I'm going to start counting from 50. When you hear me at your depth, say 'I'm here, Emma'. 50, 51, 52, 53, 54 . . .

'RICHARD': It's no use. Too late, Emma. Rick! Wait for me! I can help you! Rick . . . !

At this point the tape records the sound of the patient in convulsion. This is followed by a loud crash as he falls to the floor, overturning his chair and the table and tape recorder.

The tape continues to record as the guards and nurse posted outside run in.

Dr Todd is heard asking what has happened. Someone says that the patient is lying unconscious, his head badly gashed.

The tape then ceased to record. It was later discovered that one of the guards had stepped on the machine.

End of Transcript

As you are aware, the patient did not regain consciousness despite X-rays showing that the injury to his head was only superficial. He died in coma seventeen days later.

I shall be happy to discuss this matter further with you on a personal basis at your convenience.

Yours sincerely,

Roger A. Killanin

TO:
Dr J. W. Dale
Randall Institute for Psychical Research
University of Oxford
England

Darling Jo,

The last three months have felt like three years. But at last the ordeal is over and the inquiry has decided that I am not to blame.

Hooray! Two cheers! Rise to the sound of one hand clapping!

You would think, wouldn't you, that it would be a weight off my mind? I should feel liberated, or at least relieved.

The fact is it scarcely touches me. I never believed I would be found guilty of negligence or unprofessional behaviour. That was not the fear that kept me awake at night, or haunted my dreams when I fell at last into a drugged, exhausted sleep. It was a very different fear, which I have had to keep to myself until now. It would certainly have blown my credibility if it had come up at the inquiry. I didn't even dare write to you, because, although I trust your discretion absolutely, these things have a way of getting out.

But now that it's over I need to talk to someone, and since

All I want you to do is read this document that I've had typed up from a tape. You will realise at once who is speaking. He picks up his story from the point where I lost him on the afternoon that he went into coma.

I will write to you again in a couple of days, by which time you will have read it – at least once, if I am not mistaken.

Love,

Emma

PART THREE

Emma, this is for you. It's only fair you should know what happened. That much I owe you.

To begin with, I was a lot less confident than I wanted to admit that it was going to work. It was only an idea, and maybe a crazy one. But it's like they say about being paranoid: it doesn't stop people plotting against you. In the same way, being crazy doesn't mean you may not be right.

The trance was no problem. Nor was the regression. And those depth reports you wanted were very useful. Having to call out numbers like that worked a little like jet thrust, pushing me back and down, helping me figure out where I was and how fast I was going.

The past flashed by like a video on rewind, only I had the feeling I was inside the picture instead of watching it on a screen. For a while I felt like a man drowning. I started to panic.

That was when I lost contact with you. And when Richard went off after Rick to rescue him. From that point on they became one.

So who am I?

Well, now, that's the question, isn't it?

Scaring him awake with that apocalyptic 'fire in the skies' scenario was pure clumsiness. I was searching around in his unconscious for something I might be able to use, when I somehow drove this thing out of the undergrowth. It was like stepping on a sleeping rabbit: I scared myself as much as I scared him.

I tried my best to get his attention when he went downstairs and looked out at the garden in the moonlight, but all

I managed was to make him want a cup of hot chocolate to soothe his nerves! Then there wasn't much I could do while he and Anne had their little scene in the kitchen and back in bed. Following which he fell into a deep sleep, and I had to lie low until Charlie came and told him that the cat was stuck on the roof.

The damn cat, of course, sensed something. That's why it lashed out at him. It sensed some alien presence – me – that scared the hell out of it.

I knew the fall was coming, so I braced myself, thinking I could maybe use the shock as a way of getting through to him. But he was too stunned to be aware of anything except the fact of his survival. The incident had scared him more than I had realised myself the first time around.

My next chance was when he looked in his mirror to shave. He was alone, still shaken up, but sufficiently recovered to be receptive. For a moment I thought I was getting through to him. He started consciously reflecting on what might have been ('Another couple of feet either way and it would have been like a coconut against concrete'). This provided an opening through which I might possibly have planted the idea in his mind that all the might-have-beens in his world were actual realities in other worlds. But then, sensing my presence unconsciously, he side-tracked the whole train of thought into that little waking nightmare about brain damage.

What I desperately needed was something that would affect what Anne did that morning. If only I could make him ask her some favour, to stop by a shop, post a letter – anything so that she would not be in her car at the time and place where the accident was due to happen.

But the idea had to seem to arise spontaneously within his own consciousness. I couldn't risk direct communication; there was no time to explain rationally everything that I would have had to explain.

The next time I came close to getting his attention was while he was driving to the office. The trouble was that

I became so engrossed in leading his thoughts the way I wanted them to go that I forgot all about the truck that was due to come barrelling around the corner. His reactions were impressive. We were both alive, but I was no closer to my goal.

After that I couldn't find a crack through which to slip even half a thought into his mind. He was so scared by this second brush with death that his concentration became super-human. His fainting spell in Crossfield's office was caused by me throwing all caution to the wind and screaming at him to listen while there was still time. He tried instinctively to shut me out, as he would a bad memory or an unseemly thought.

He knew at that moment – I know he knew! – that something in his head was urging him to call Anne, to make an excuse, any excuse, to prevent her going out in her car with Charlie that morning. And yet he wouldn't listen.

It was understandable, of course. And yet I would like to think that I, in his position, would have shown a little less rigidity and a little more imagination.

But how can I be sure? Did I ever, before this happened, really trust my imagination? We tend to think of it as no more than a distorting mirror of reality, a screen upon which cheap fantasies can be projected. How wrong we are. Imagination is the door to everything.

I knew that my last chance was in the men's room. By the time he got into the meeting and started doodling on his pad, it would be too late. I knew that I had to hit him with everything I had right there while he was dowsing his face with water and wondering what was wrong with him.

What I didn't know was how much I had to hit him with, or precisely what form it would take. I wasn't any more ready than he was for what actually happened.

Emma, this is new ground. This is where you lost 'Richard' as well as 'Rick' – because Rick needed all the help he could get. This is where this whole identity thing gets really mixed up.

He – the old Rick; the, if you like, original – was feeling like shit and looking at himself in the mirror wondering what the hell was wrong and (you'll remember this from what I wrote before) he gets the feeling that something is behind him and he whips around. There was nothing there the first time.

But this time . . . oh, boy!

I was there!

He stared. What little colour he had left in his face drained clear away and I thought he was about to pass out.

Frankly, I didn't feel too great myself. I didn't know how I'd got there. Will power? Desperation? Was I really there at all?

I could feel the floor under my feet and I could see my reflection in the mirror behind him.

I was wearing Richard's clothes!

And I had – I can't explain this, maybe you can – I had this great gash on my forehead, like I'd been hit, or I'd fallen. But hard. It looked nasty. Does that mean anything to you?

Anyway, there I was, feeling as surprised to be there as he was to see me. But I had the edge on him – just. I grabbed him by the wrist and said: 'Don't ask questions! Just come with me.'

You may ask why did I have to drag him along. Wouldn't it have been simpler just to get into a car – any car – and take care of things myself? I knew where Anne was. I could have gone straight there without having to argue with him all the way, without having him maybe do something stupid and ruin everything. Why didn't I do that?

The answer is I don't know. I'm not even sure that I consciously thought about it at the time. What I do know is what I felt. And what I felt was that I was in some strange way bound to him. I knew at that moment that I was real to him, but I didn't know whether I'd be equally real to Anne. I couldn't be sure that if I tried to run out of there on my own and tell her not to drive her car that morning . . . I couldn't be sure that she'd even know that I was there, let alone listen to me. And I didn't have time to find out.

'Don't pass out!' I said, my first words to him. (I could say my first words to myself, but why complicate matters?) 'I can't explain,' I went on, 'at least not now. Anne's in danger. She'll die if you don't come with me.'

He – thank God, or Whatever – was too shaken to give me an argument. It was all he could do to stay on his feet and control the speed at which his head was spinning. He looked like his mouth wouldn't work. Or maybe his brain. Or both.

'Don't panic, it's all right,' I said, several times. I wanted to shout but didn't know if the others would be able to hear me or not through the door, so I kept my voice down. 'I'm going mad!' he said. His hands had gone up to his head, like he was trying to keep his skull from splitting open.

'You're not going mad,' I told him. 'What's happening is going to take a lot of understanding, but you *will* understand it. Right now we've got to get out of here.'

I looked around for a way. We could have just raced through Crossfield's office, but I didn't want to risk the tangle. Can you imagine? One guy goes to the can and comes out twins.

Or, equally undesirable, even if the others couldn't see me, they'd see him looking like a man demented and send for security!

There was a good-sized window, steel-framed, partially open. I pushed it and looked out. 'There's a ledge. We can crawl along it to the fire escape. Come on!'

He still didn't move. I grabbed him by the shoulders and shook him. 'Don't think about it! Just *do* it! It's Anne's life!'

His eyes searched mine. I saw raw fear in them. 'I know,' I said. 'It's impossible, but it's happening. You're not going mad, and you're not dreaming. But Anne is going to be crushed to death in an automobile accident in half an hour. I've been trying to warn you since you woke up in the middle of the night. Everything that's been happening has been me. Do you understand what I'm saying?'

He nodded dumbly, as though something, somehow, was getting through to him. I half pulled, half pushed him out the window and on to the ledge. He was starting to shake, and for one awful moment I thought he was going to lose it right there – four floors above a small courtyard of solid concrete.

'Get a grip!' I hissed back at him, struggling to turn and make a grab if he keeled over. He took a deep breath, closed his eyes, then nodded that he was all right. At least he didn't suffer from vertigo. That much I knew for a fact – from the inside.

We didn't exchange more than three words until we were down the fire escape. The last section of it made so much noise as it swung down that I thought we were certain to be caught. In fact only one person looked out to see what was going on – Crossfield's assistant, Gaines, appeared at the window we'd just climbed out of. Luckily he didn't see me – I'd just stepped into the shadow of a doorway. But he called out, 'Rick, what the hell are you doing?'

Rick looked up, made a sort of vague gesture, didn't know what to answer. 'Come on,' I said. 'The garage.' He followed me into the darkness.

'Give me your keys.' He fumbled in his pockets and handed them over. My own keys to my own car.

He didn't take his eyes off me as I started her up, backed out of the visitor space, and swung around for the exit. I felt my face crease in a smile. I couldn't help it.

'You're looking at me like I'm a ghost,' I said. 'Maybe I am. I'm a little unsure about my exact status – but I'm here.'

'How . . . ?'

'Many Worlds theory. It's all true. Everett was right.'

'I don't . . . '

'Of course you don't. Who would?'

'But why . . . ?'

'Because if Anne dies, you make a leap into a parallel universe. And believe me, we can all do without what follows.'

'But how come you . . . ?'

'I time travelled. Used hypnotic regression to get back into my own head. *Your* head.'

'But you're not in my head.'

'Don't assume. Don't assume anything.'

He was silent for a moment, finally taking his eyes off me and looking out at the world flashing by. 'Where are we going?'

'The accident happens on Pilgrim Hill. She's going up and there's this rig coming down. I figure if we cut through Fishergate we can intercept her before she gets there.'

Again he hesitated a moment before speaking. His eyes flickered my way, and again I saw fear in them. But a different sort of fear this time.

'Will it work?'

'I know it will.' I didn't feel as confident as I tried to sound, but what else was I going to say?

He continued to look at me. 'What happened to you? How did you get that cut on your head?'

I fingered the cut, looked at the blood on my hand. I'd forgotten about it.

'I don't know,' I said. I looked down at my clothes. They were the clothes I'd been wearing in prison. But I didn't know how I got that cut. It worried me. I don't know why, but I felt there was something wrong. Still, I didn't have time to vex about it then.

We made good time through the traffic. I jumped no lights and took no risks. The last thing I wanted was a siren and a cop waving me – us – over.

Rick, the 'old' Rick, remained quiet. He was reacting just as I hoped I would have to a seemingly impossible situation: ask a few critical questions, then stay calm and let things unfold.

'You didn't tell me about Charlie,' he said after a while. 'Is Charlie in the car with her?'

'Yes, he is. But he's strapped in the back seat, as always, and comes out without a scratch. Anne's the one who takes the full impact.'

He fell silent again. Then: 'What do we do when we see her?'

'We stop her!'

'Then what? Do we both get out and tell her what you've just told me?'

'Let's worry about that later. Right now let's just find her.'

I looked at my watch. In a moment we'd be nearing the foot of Pilgrim Hill. She couldn't possibly have got there yet, so I figured that if we pulled on to the hard shoulder and waited we'd be in good time to stop her.

'We can't just park here,' he said. 'You know what the cops are like. If they see us . . .'

'I know.' I reached under the dash to release the hood. 'Pretend you're working on the engine. I'll watch the road.'

'We'll *both* watch the road,' he said.

'Okay – but not standing there like Tweedledum and Tweedledee, or she'll freak!'

He ducked under the open hood, peering around the edge, while I stood by the road scanning the two lanes of cars that were approaching the long, curving gradient up Pilgrim Hill.

I checked my watch again. She should be coming into view any second. I couldn't see her.

A shiver went down my spine. Could I have got it wrong? Was there any other direction she could have been coming from? I raced through all the possibilities, but couldn't think of one. Aside from she'd been going down the hill and made an illegal U-turn. But she wouldn't do that. She was a careful driver. And with Charlie in the car . . . !

Then I saw her. The pale green Deux Chevaux was in the

180

outside lane between two other cars. A truck was coming up on the inside lane, and I suddenly realised that if I didn't move fast it was going to block our view.

I shouted. 'She's there! Quick!'

He took in the situation at a glance, and started running in the direction of the traffic to try and catch her as she came around the truck.

But her lane slowed and the inside one kept moving. I ran against the traffic, waving furiously, shouting. She didn't see me.

Then her lane picked up speed and she disappeared from my view. I looked at the other Rick. He'd realised what was happening and was jumping up and down waving his arms. Suddenly a smaller van in front of the truck blocked his view. He started to run, one way, then another, finally diving into the traffic and triggering an angry blaring of horns.

It was no good. She was past and we'd missed her! To my alarm, I realised that the truck was pulling in. I saw it was a breakdown truck. The driver had seen our hood up and was signalling an offer of help.

The other Rick was already racing back towards me, white with fear, screaming something I couldn't make out. He slammed down the Mustang's hood and wrenched open the door.

The keys were in the ignition and he was already behind the wheel and gunning the engine when I leapt in alongside him. We almost skinned the driver of the breakdown truck as he was climbing from his cab. I looked around and saw him yelling something and giving us the finger, but he was unhurt.

Rick swung the car into the traffic without looking. He was hunched over the wheel and oblivious of the renewed blaring of horns and the wrenching of metal as we took somebody's front fender and lost our own rear one.

'Take it easy,' I yelled. 'We want to get there.'

He didn't answer. His eyes were staring like a madman's. I hung on to the dashboard and the door as he wove in and

181

out of the traffic with no regard to his own or anyone else's safety.

A kind of lassitude came over me. I don't know if it was a reaction to fear, or just simply that my energies were spent. I'd come this far, and now things were out of my control. I felt myself fading, as if I were no longer wholly there.

The pale green Citroen came into view a few cars ahead, still in the outside lane and slowing as the climb steepened.

'There she is!' I pointed.

He had already seen her, and was pumping his horn and grinding gears as he tried to force a way between the two lanes. It didn't work.

I gave a yell of alarm as he swung back into the outside lane, making a beat-up old Chevy brake so hard that it was rear-ended by the car behind.

Suddenly we were speeding up the middle of the highway, straddling the centre line, heading into a long, blind turn against fast traffic coming down.

I cried out. 'For Christ's sake watch out! It happens just here . . . '

Then, just as we drew level with Anne's car, I saw it – the truck that was going to kill her. It was going fast, too fast, but it seemed to be under control. For a moment I thought it wasn't going to happen. I thought we were going to get away with it.

Then, for no reason I could see, the truck swerved towards us, its rig coming around with a terrible slow-motion effect, starting to jack-knife.

Then the impact!

I felt myself hurtling through the air, and everything went black.

When I came to, I was lying by the roadside and somebody was putting something soft under my head. I looked around.

There were no cops or ambulances, but the traffic was stopped in both directions and people were crowding out of the vehicles to see what had happened. Obviously I'd only been unconscious for a few seconds.

I couldn't see Anne. I didn't know whether she and Charlie had escaped the crash, or whether we'd all finished up in it together – the truck, the Mustang, and her Citroen. For all I knew, I might have just made things worse by my meddling and killed Charlie, too.

Then I saw them. She was carrying Charlie in her arms and pushing through the crowd towards me. She looked stricken, as though she'd seen the whole thing and was sure I must be dead.

But then she saw my eyes open, looking at her. I saw her give a little cry of relief. I couldn't hear it, but I knew how it sounded. This was Anne. *My* Anne! I knew the sound that came from her throat when her lips moved like that.

She ran to my side, still holding Charlie, and knelt by me.

'Rick, my darling! Are you all right?'

'I'm fine,' I said. I felt my neck move. And my head. I shifted my legs a fraction. I wasn't paralysed.

'Lie still. There's an ambulance on its way. Oh, Rick, what on earth were you doing . . . ?'

She had put Charlie down and was dabbing at a cut on my head. Charlie was holding on to her, silent and wide-eyed with fear and incomprehension.

'Everything's okay, Charlie. Don't be scared,' I told him.

But at the back of my mind a dreadful question was starting to hammer at me like a migraine.

Where was Charlie's 'other' father? Anne's 'other' husband?

Was he still in the car? Buried in the wreckage?

Dead? Alive?

Had no one found him yet?

What would happen when they did? What would I say?

From the moment I found myself standing in that washroom with my identical twin, I hadn't thought any further forward than preventing the accident. I certainly hadn't thought about what Anne was going to do with two husbands. Or Charlie with two fathers.

I suppose that, in some instinctive way, I figured that those kind of logical contradictions were impossible. They couldn't be sensibly thought about, therefore they couldn't happen.

Wasn't that what Tickelbakker had said? 'Anything possible can happen. But not anything conceivable.'

Was it possible that the laws of physics would allow such an absurdity?

But then they seemed already to have allowed it. There had been two of us.

I heard sirens, running feet, the voices of authority. A moment later I was surrounded by cops and paramedics.

'What about the other guy?' I said. 'How is he?'

The paramedic looked alarmed, like he'd missed something vital. 'What other guy?'

'In the car. The one who was driving.'

A cop loomed over us. 'There was nobody else in that car, buddy. *You* were driving. We'll talk about that later. Now get him to the hospital.'

I didn't argue. Warning lights were going on in my brain. Stay quiet, I told myself. Don't make the same mistake twice. Take your time, let things unfold. Don't give them any excuse to call you crazy.

It was then, as they lifted me on to the stretcher, that I looked down at the rest of my body. I only caught a glimpse as they were wrapping a blanket around me, but it was enough.

Emma, if you ever get this, you're not going to believe it. But you *are* going to get it. And in some way that will *make* you believe it.

I'll find a way. I know I can do it. Because now I know – really know – that anything's possible.

Anything.

What I saw, Emma, when I looked down at myself, was this:

I was wearing his clothes.

Let me try and make this absolutely clear. At the moment the accident happened, the Rick/Richard that you knew, and whom I have been referring to as 'I', was wearing the clothes that Richard had been wearing in jail: blue jeans and a thick grey sweater.

Rick — the Rick we had come back to warn — was wearing a dark business suit that morning, with a pink shirt and a tie in red and black and with a touch of blue.

And that's what I found myself looking down at as they lifted me on to the stretcher.

The suit, the shirt and tie were torn and smeared with blood and dirt, but they were *his clothes*!

And I was in them.

So who the hell was 'I' now?

'Rick . . . ?'

'Mmmm . . . ?'

'I don't believe you.'

'I can't help that.'

We were in bed back at Long Chimneys. Miraculously, I only had a few cuts and bruises, and they let me go home that night.

'But . . . '

I kissed her.

'Don't interrupt.'

'Sorry. You were saying.'

'Believing it in theory isn't the same as believing it for real.'

I sighed and stroked her hair, pulling her closer. 'You know what I think?' I said. 'I don't think it's important.'

'How can you say that?' She looked up at me, and there was a note of protest in her voice. 'You abandon your meeting at the bank, climb out of a window so they'll probably think you're a lunatic and never lend you another penny — and all because you had this sudden "feeling" that I was going to have an accident.'

'A feeling that was strong enough', I reminded her, 'to take me to exactly the spot where you happened to be, and which I couldn't have possibly known about – and at exactly the moment that a truck burst a tyre and jackknifed in the road. Now, if you've any other explanations besides telepathy, I'd like to hear them.'

She was silent. We made love again. There was nothing more to say.

Be honest, Emma. What would you have done in my place? Tell the truth? I doubt it.

I'd given things a lot of thought in the ambulance and in the hospital. Finally I came to a conclusion:

I am whoever I want to be.

And I *want* to be Charlie's father and Anne's husband. Here, in this life, where everything is just the way it was – with one exception.

Me.

But that's my secret. No one will ever know.

Anyway, I couldn't tell the truth even if I wanted to. You see, no one ever saw the two of us together. Not even the driver of the breakdown truck. He saw only one man at the roadside, and one man driving off like a lunatic.

Don't ask me how all this can be. It just is.

I'd rather be accused of driving like a lunatic than sounding like one.

Actually, Emma, there's something else that I can't tell anyone but you.

I've learned how to do it at will.

Leap universes.

Weeeeeee-eeeeee-eeeee-eeee-eee!!!

It's amazing.

You remember how I said to Tickelbakker that maybe the human mind was capable of doing for itself all the weird stuff that it dreams up? He thought I was losing it, suffering from shock, so I didn't push the point.

But I was serious. And now I've proved it.

Emma, I've been visiting other universes. Once you've done it a couple of times, it's relatively easy. You don't need to be hypnotised. You don't even have to meditate. All it takes is a moment's concentration. Of a very special kind, admittedly. But it's not difficult. My technique isn't perfect yet and I sometimes miss the target universe. But I've learned something very important:

You can't change anything.

All you can do is transplant yourself into one of the alternatives.

For instance, this universe that I'm in now, the one I use as home base, is not the same as the one in which Anne dies. It branches off from that one at the point where 'I' get back and confront myself in the washroom at the bank. From that moment on, I'm in a different universe. Everything in it is different, even if only minutely. This is the universe where Anne does not die.

Correction, *one* of the universes where she does not die. The Anne who survives is as close to the other Anne — my Anne — as a clone, but she's not the same Anne.

And that other universe, the one where Anne dies, is still there. I'm still a widower looking after Charlie in it. I still have the dream of becoming part of Richard again and killing Anne and Harold. But, in that universe, I wake up from it. It's just a bad dream.

And they do fine — that Rick and Charlie. I stayed in his head just long enough to be sure. He gets over the Emma thing in a month or two, and even agrees to be Harold's best man at the wedding. That's partly because by then he's met a girl who . . . but that's another story.

The point I'm making, Emma, is that you can never get back to where you were. Even if I got back into the 'me' that you were dealing with on that day when I died, from that moment on 'we' would be in a different universe,

187

you and I, with a different 'me' and a different 'you'. Only marginally different. But all the same, different.

That's the one frustration. You can't go back. The universe you want to change goes on just the way it would have – except that 'would have' is a distortion caused by a language that was neither formed out of, nor is capable of dealing with, the reality I am talking about.

God, Emma, I know that in shrink talk these are the ravings of a madman. But you're different. That's why I want to tell you all this. (If only I could. Incidentally, Emma, in one universe you and I are married. In another we're lovers. There's one where we ... but no, that must be 'their' little secret.)

By the way, there's another thing I want to tell you. I've now learned how to move backwards and forwards in time – not as far in either direction as I'd like yet, but I'm improving. I think, if I wanted to, I could spend weeks, months or even years in one of my other lives, then return to home base where no time at all had passed. If I kept on doing it, it would be a form of immortality. Almost. But I'm not sure I want that. Left to themselves, all the versions of me will come to their natural end. Maybe that's how I'll leave them.

Still, for the moment, I'm enjoying the travelling. Some of the small differences between neighbouring universes can be interesting, but they can also get boring after a while. It's a little like an endless game of Trivial Pursuit. You know – who got the Vivien Leigh role in that 'other' version of *Gone With The Wind*? Or who was president in place of Jimmy Carter? Who cares? And it doesn't make a lot of difference.

But some of the more distant universes ... now they are extraordinary!

I think I've glimpsed Heaven. I know I've had a whiff of Hell.

They exist.

There is no 'Time'.

All things *are* contained within a grain of sand.
Many suspect these things are true.
But I *know*. I have seen and touched them.
Yet I always come back to Anne and Charlie.
And they never know I've been away.

Anne will be having the baby soon. I'm excited about that. Of course, I realise that he's (we know it's a boy) not entirely my son. Genetically, yes. But he's the son of the man Anne married, and I am – in a sense – someone else.

But I mustn't let myself dwell on that. When I find this depressing sense of secret alienation beginning to envelop me, I go on my travels again.

On the whole I stick now to a fairly small circle of other universes and other selves. These are all versions of what I call the 'essential me'. I suppose in a sense I've created them. They all branch off from various aspects of the me I was when I first talked to you. So in a sense they're all alienated from their worlds in the way I am from mine, which is comforting.

We're like friends popping into one another's houses without knocking. Our lives are so nearly identical that we amuse ourselves by comparing minute differences of detail. For instance, last Tuesday one of us sneezed at breakfast, but nobody else did. That was the only difference we could find.

Imagine, a whole universe hanging on a sneeze.

Sometimes, Emma, it's only thoughts like that that keep me sane.

I'm very tired now, Emma. I've finally reached you, but it wasn't easy.

The next question is, how am I going to make you believe me?

I think I know how.

Reach out and touch me, Emma. Reach out and touch my face.

Now . . .

POSTSCRIPT

Jo darling,

So there you have it. You've read it — and the obvious question you're asking yourself is, if Hamilton never regained consciousness before he died, how did I get all that stuff? When did he talk to me?

Well, the truth is that he did regain consciousness, in a sort of way. Only I knew, and I couldn't tell anybody because of the sort of way that it was.

You remember that Hamilton was in coma for seventeen days. During that time I visited him frequently because, inevitably, I felt at least partly responsible for what had happened. I had taken a certain risk, albeit in the interest of helping my patient, but it had gone badly. I felt obliged to do everything I could to salvage the situation.

The day I'm talking about was the seventeenth day of his coma, the day he finally died. It was a Monday. I'd been in the hospital for my usual clinic, and afterwards I stopped by Hamilton's room. I sat there talking to him the same way I'd been doing since it happened, playing some of the tapes we'd made in his earlier sessions, going over what we'd talked about, trying to find that line between coma and trance and bring him back. I suppose I didn't expect any more success than usual, because when the time came to go and I heard some kind of movement, I just assumed there must be somebody else in the room with us — somebody who must have been there the whole time, because I hadn't heard them come in.

I felt it was kind of creepy that they'd just been there, listening, saying nothing, not moving all that time. I called out, 'Who's there?' But nobody answered.

I asked again. Still no reply. And then I heard a voice say, 'Emma . . . ?'

It was his voice. Weak, but unmistakably his voice. He was out of the coma.

'Richard?' I said. No reaction. So I tried, 'Rick?'

I heard him chuckle. 'Whichever,' he said.

'How are you feeling?'

'Oh . . . that's a little difficult to describe.' There was something in his voice – I don't know how to put it – as though he was somehow *amused* by the whole situation.

Then he said something very strange. He said, 'It took me a while to figure out how I got that crack on the head.'

That made me think. He hurt his head when he fell, but that happened when he was in deep trance. It was a relatively superficial injury – a consequence of going into coma, not the cause of it.

Suddenly I heard him chuckle again, as though he knew what I was thinking.

'You're wondering', he said, 'how a guy in a coma knows he's got a crack on the head? That's part of what I'm here to tell you, Emma. Have you got that little tape recorder of yours?'

'Yes.'

'You'd better switch it on.'

I felt for the bedside table where I'd put it and pressed record.

'Is it running?' he asked.

I told him it was. And he began. 'Emma, this is for you. It's only fair you should know what happened. That much I owe you . . . '

You have read the rest, right down to: 'Reach out and touch me, Emma. Reach out and touch my face . . . '

I did. I reached out . . . and I felt for the bed . . . and I felt my way up to his face . . . and I touched him.

And I knew right away that he was dead.

I checked his pulse, though I knew there was no point. Later we were able to determine at exactly what time his heart had stopped. He had been dead a full twelve minutes before I entered that room. I had been talking to a dead man.

But that wasn't possible. I had the tape. I could prove what had happened. Other people would hear it.

I rewound it. And listened.

The words were exactly the words I had heard, the words you have read. 'Emma, this is for you. It's only fair you should know what happened.' And so on.

The only thing different was the voice.

It was my voice.

Of course I couldn't believe it, and simply didn't believe it at first. I fast-forwarded, rewound, skimmed the tape back and forth from end to end, persuading myself that I would find his voice somewhere if only I searched hard enough.

But in the end there was no escaping the truth. I had hallucinated. I had heard his voice in my head, but the voice that spoke his words was my own.

I fought my panic. I could feel reality giving way under my feet.

Just suppose, I said, just suppose for the sake of argument that all that stuff about parallel worlds, and about his learning to hop between them, just suppose that was all true. Given that, then getting into my head, as he'd got into Richard's, wouldn't have been all that unlikely.

But even allowing that it was possible, why would he do it?

To show it could be done, yes. But why was he so keen to show *me*? Out of gratitude, like he said? 'That much I owe you'?

Maybe.

Or maybe he was just damned if he would let me *not* believe him. He knew that half of me was rationalising everything he said and writing him off as deluded, while the other half of me was strangely tempted to believe.

It was true. I'd had this feeling from the first time I

met him that there was something unnervingly plausible about him. I've known cases of logorrhea fantastica that would convince even the most sophisticated casual listener, but which I would spot in a second for what they were.

Hamilton was different. Don't ask how. Somehow. It was almost as if there was a contest between us. He would win if he could persuade me that he was telling the truth and wasn't just sick. I would win if, in the end, I remained convinced that he was sick.

So how was he going to persuade me? If he'd had somebody else come to me with a message in their head from him, I'd have dismissed them as 'sick', too. I could have rationalised away just about any method he used to contact me. Except this one.

This I could not dismiss. He was betting that my sanity was the most important thing I had. After all, I was a psychiatrist. I worked on other people's minds, made judgments about them. What would happen if I had to make a judgment about my own? Surely I would be able to satisfy myself that I was sane; and then, he must have reasoned, I would believe him.

Do I?

I don't know. I don't know if I know anything any more. For the first time in my life, I am truly in the dark.

Emma